McGivern

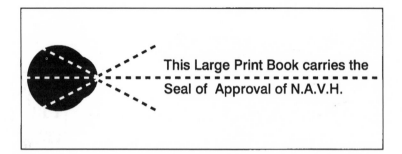

This Large Print Book carries the
Seal of Approval of N.A.V.H.

McGivern

T. V. Olsen

G.K. Hall & Co. • Thorndike, Maine

Published in 2001 by arrangement with Golden West Literary Agency.

G.K. Hall Large Print Western Series.

The text of this Large Print edition is unabridged.
Other aspects of the book may vary from the original edition.

Set in 16 pt. Plantin by Christina S. Huff.

Printed in the United States on permanent paper.

Library of Congress Cataloging-in-Publication Data

Olsen, Theodore V.
      McGivern : a Western novel / by T. V. Olsen.
         p.   cm.
       ISBN 0-7838-9412-0 (lg. print : hc : alk. paper)
      1. Illegal arms transfers — Fiction.   2. Apache Indians — Wars
      — Fiction.   3. Texas — Fiction.   4. Large type books.
      I. Title.
PS3565.L8 M36   2001
      813´.54—dc21

00-143880

1

The Douherty Wagon lay on its side, blackened ribs already partly submerged in the loose sand whipped along by hot air currents from up-canyon. A dozen yards beyond lay the charred body of the stagecoach. McGivern swung down from his line-backed dun, walked stiff-legged to the coach, and stared at it for a measureless time. He turned away, squinted eyes scanning the ground. He hadn't supposed he'd find anything. The detail from Fort Laughlin had scoured the canyon thoroughly, and the wind would by now have obliterated all sign of the massacre. Even a trained scout would find nothing.

The high cliffs of red sandstone that walled the gorge caught the sunglare, shimmered part of it skyward in transparent waves, and reflected the rest, angrily beating it against McGivern's body. Mechanically he shucked off his coat — fine black broadcloth, splotched now with white alkali muddied by sweat stains — and fastened it behind his saddle.

He remained by his horse, one arm slung across the saddle swell, aware at last of the crushing exhaustion of these long hours of rocking in the saddle at a deadly pace with the contained thoughts of a madman. *So this is how it ends,* he thought detachedly. *Nothing.* Nothing but the mute token of the charred coach, a broadcloth wedding suit — a now-limp, now-grimy symbol of plans that would never materialize — and his tired mind trying to pull nightmare fragments of memory into some kind of meaning. . . .

Yesterday he had risen as usual in the bachelor's quarters behind his freight yard at Silver City. Only this morning was different . . . his last one in these lonely rooms. Today Ann was arriving on the noon stage. The new house he'd built on the edge of town was furnished and ready. The town hall had been engaged for the afternoon ceremony, with Parson Negley, circuit preacher, officiating, and all of McGivern's friends — teamsters, miners, and their families — turning out for a shivaree.

McGivern had bathed and shaved with extra care, put on his new suit and stepped out to his office. There he collided with the white-haired agent from the telegraph office. The old man was out of breath; wordlessly he handed McGivern the yellow sheet of paper that sent him on a dead run for the stables, throwing his hull on his best saddle mount and kicking the animal savagely into motion before he was securely in leather.

It was a mistake. No wedding joke could be this cruel, so it had to be a mistake. That was the frenzied conviction that kept churning in his mind through the long hours that followed, as he drove his exhausted sorrel along the western trail from Silver City. And knowing all the while, in the back of his mind, that Colonel Dudley C. Cahill, commandant at Fort Laughlin, didn't make that kind of mistake.

By late afternoon he'd reached the fort. The orderly had ushered him into the C.O.'s office, and Cahill had given him the whole story.

A band of young Chiricahua bucks, fired by two rebellious war chiefs, had broken off San Carlos Reservation a month ago and drifted south, cutting a two-hundred-mile swath of lightning raids, striking at widely isolated points. The route leading to Fort Laughlin from the east fell inside that swath. Within a single week, two stages on the Butterfield Overland line had been attacked — the teams driven off, the coaches overturned and burned, and the bodies of drivers and passengers riddled with arrows.

With this grim precedent as a warning, the stage which had rolled out for Fort Laughlin two days ago had joined forces with an Army paymaster's wagon heading in the same direction. The Douherty paywagon had been accompanied by a detail of ten mounted troopers, which should have been enough to discourage an attack. Yet when they entered Creagh Canyon, where the road wended between towering walls, the Apaches had struck.

"Yesterday," Colonel Cahill had told Mc-Givern, "when the stage and the payroll detail were six hours overdue at the fort, I sent out a patrol under Lieutenant Kearny, accompanied by an ambulance wagon. When they returned this morning, it was with a wagonful of — bodies. There were no survivors. The troopers . . . the stage passengers . . . all . . ."

One of the bodies was that of a woman, still clutching a torn reticule. In it the colonel had found a letter from Tom McGivern of Silver City, addressed to Miss Ann Fulverton of Nealtown, Ohio. The colonel had at once dispatched a telegram to McGivern, whom he knew.

McGivern's memories after that were confused. There had been the brutal, necessary job of identification. He had seen the ugly aftermath of massacre before, but never in this personal, shocking manner. A quick lance thrust had killed Ann; he was thankful only for the swiftness of her death.

The next morning he threw his saddle on a borrowed Army mount and headed east for Creagh Canyon to view the scene for himself, with a vague hope that he could turn up something; he had no idea what.

Nor did he have any idea now, leaning on the dun's sweat-frothed flank in the oppressive heat, staring at the wrecks of stage and paywagon and the blank floor of the canyon. Mostly the impulse that brought him here had been a need to move, to try to outride the crazy grief that left him numb and wondering.

A hot breath of wind launched stinging sand against his face, arousing him. He turned to mount and begin the long ride back to the fort. As he started to swing his left foot to stirrup, his toe struck something covered by an inch of earth. He stooped and brushed away the loose sand, down to a gleam of metal. He tugged and the object lifted easily.

A rifle. A shiny new '73 Winchester repeater. The Army didn't supply its men with such guns. It might have belonged to a stage passenger . . . or else, the Apaches. . . . Swift anger touched McGivern as he turned the rifle in his hands. If the Chiricahuas had been armed with new Winchesters, it was little wonder they'd dared to attack a large party of whites.

The anger was biting and welcome, scouring into his apathy and grief. He shoved the rifle into his empty saddle boot, swung astride the dun and turned its head for Fort Laughlin. He was erect in the saddle now, his face set stonily.

2

Colonel Dudley C. Cahill signed the last of a batch of quartermaster's requisitions, threw down his pen with a grunt of relief, and called to his secretary-orderly. The corporal stepped in from the outer office, took the bundle of papers from the colonel's desk, tapped them neatly into alignment, and hesitated.

"Well, Haney?"

"McGivern just rode through the stockade gate. . . . I guess he's back, sir," the corporal ended feebly.

"Astute observation," the colonel said dryly. "Suppose you spend more time with your filing, less looking out the window. McGivern will be over directly. Show him in."

"Yes, sir." His sallow face flushed, the corporal retreated to the outer office.

The colonel sighed, stretched his arms, shoved back his swivel chair and walked to the window to stare across the parade grounds drowsing in the quiet of deepening dusk. A pair of troopers were gossiping apathetically on the sutler's porch. A hot breath of wind brushed up a spume of dust and passed on through the window to stir the colonel's thin white hair. He was a fleshy, dour-faced man with a cold cigar clamped in his bulldog jaws, a man who had spent most of his fifty-five years in the service, all of the sixteen since the end of the Civil War in the Army of the West.

A trickle of sweat coasted down his ribs beneath his faded blue blouse, and he cursed around his cigar. Damn this country. A man never stopped sweating. He smiled thinly, then. Arizona grew on a man — the same way Hell would, he supposed; yet he liked the land and its people — even the savage Apache foe he'd engaged so often. He liked it all, except for the scum who were a part of neither side, who plied their intrigues between Indian and white, stirring up every dormant tension . . . the territorial politicians, the treaty breakers . . . and the lower echelons of scum, the whiskey-and-gun runners.

God wither all their seed, the colonel thought wearily, feeling the deep-rutted futility of his position. He was Army, a mere link in a vast hierarchy of command. In his way, he felt the same boredom as the corporal. At times he wished he were a free agent who could smash the scum he had to protect, though it meant a continuation of their hate-mongering plots.

A free agent like Tom McGivern.

The colonel felt a twinge of guilt, thinking of the plan that had rooted in his mind after McGivern had left the fort yesterday. A man like McGivern would want revenge. The colonel meant to give that urge direction. Indirectly he

13

would be taking advantage of McGivern's deep grief, better healed and forgotten as soon as possible. But the stakes were large, involving many lives.

He saw McGivern leave the stables now and slant across the parade grounds toward his office, drag-footed with weariness. Pity touched the colonel; he hoped wryly that he could keep the justification he had given himself topmost in his mind during the next fifteen minutes.

He walked back to his desk, sat, and leaned his elbows on the desk, steepling his fingers and staring morosely through them at the door. "Colonel Cahill is expecting you, Mr. McGivern," he heard the corporal say. McGivern tramped in, closed the inner office door, toed a chair out of the corner, swung it around facing the colonel's desk, and slacked into it. He leaned a rifle he was carrying against the desk. The colonel watched him a moment in silence, remembering what he knew of this man.

For six years, Tom McGivern had been Chief of Scouts at this fort. Before that, he had worked cows, bossed Texas trail herds until the railroad hand ended the drover days; then he prospected for gold around Tombstone, once performing the incredible feat of living alone for three months in hostile Apache country, matching his desertcraft against the wily Chiricahuas and Mescaleros while he panned and dug for gold, sometimes almost under their noses. Later he'd used this knowledge against them when

14

he'd guided the troops that had rounded up roving bands of hostiles and reservation breakaways. To cap it, McGivern had once lived for a year with the Apaches at San Carlos, learning their language, and hashing over old exploits with the very warriors he had fought.

Three years ago he had taken the accumulated savings of his prospecting and Army pay and had bought a thriving freight business in Silver City. The colonel had heard little of him since then — until yesterday, when he'd found a letter on the body of an Apache-murdered woman . . . a girl who had come hundreds of miles to marry Tom McGivern. It was old friendship that had prompted the colonel to instant dispatch of a telegram to McGivern.

Looking at him now, the colonel saw a tall and rawhide-spare man, heavy through the chest and shoulders, his Indian-dark hair streaked with gray under a dust-colored Stetson, his white linen shirt patched with sweat and dust. McGivern's lean, leathery face was composed and sober, with brown-to-amber eyes weather-tracked at the outer corners by the slight squint of a man perpetually watchful. It was a face which — Indian-like — showing nothing. But the colonel remembered that letter to Ann Fulverton, the careful, painful scrawl of a shy and lonely man. Even with his friends McGivern had always been reserved, but with her he had held back nothing.

Knowing it makes my job that much worse, the

colonel thought, but he drew a deep breath and plunged, speaking quietly:

"Hate the 'Paches, Mac?"

McGivern was brooding at the floor, his long legs outstretched, his arms folded. The colonel wondered if he'd heard. Then McGivern looked up. "Hate a whole tribe, Dud? After living with them, knowing the best of them, knowing how they've been put upon by us whites?"

"Not even after —"

McGivern's head swung up angrily. "You know as well as me where the blame goes."

The colonel exhaled slowly, nodded. "Approximately." Here was a man. McGivern hadn't lost his cool perspective, even in his stunned grief.

McGivern reached down and picked up the Winchester repeater, hefting it in his big fist. "I found this in Creagh Canyon. Your men missed it. This is what I mean, Dud. Your Army regulation rifle is the .45-.70 Springfield. A good gun within its limits. Steel-barreled, deadly up to six hundred yards. But a single-shot." McGivern laid the Winchester on the desk, tapping it with his forefinger. "The War Department should have learned something from the Little Big Horn. Custer's men all had single-shot Springfields. . . . About five hundred of the Sioux had Winchester repeaters like this one. Lever action is so smooth you get off all fifteen loads in as many seconds."

McGivern's chair creaked as he let his bulk ease back again, his words slapping at the colonel like padded clubs. "Since we got to rob, cheat, push the Indian into fighting back, you'd think we'd at least arm the cavalry so they could make a decent show. And maybe. . . ."

"Yes," the colonel said softly. "Maybe your girl would be alive. And those troopers. And a lot of people we'll never know. But the question remains: exactly where do you set the blame?"

McGivern shrugged stonily. "You can't pinpoint it. These Winchesters are used everywhere by civilians. The Indians can pick them up from greasy-thumbed traders, massacred wagon trains, murdered settlers. . . ."

The colonel stood, circled the desk with his hands folded behind his back. "Maybe we *can* pinpoint this last atrocity, Mac."

McGivern looked up with a flicker of interest. He said nothing, just waited.

The colonel swung to face him. "From time to time there've been survivors of this late series of raids. They all agreed on one thing: this bunch — numbering between thirty and forty 'Paches — were all armed with repeating rifles."

"All?" McGivern echoed, alert now. "They didn't pick up that many rifles at random."

"Something else: the payroll chest was gone from the Douherty wagon. Why? White man's money means nothing to hostiles."

McGivern leaned forward with a scowl, lacing his hands around his knee. "You think they staged this last raid just to get the Army payroll?"

17

"To pay off the white men who supplied them with the guns. We," he laid an official emphasis on the word, "believe that someone has turned gun-running into big business."

McGivern was silent for a time. Then: "Tell me all you know about this band, Dud."

The colonel walked back to his desk, sank into his chair with a sigh. "Not much, I'm afraid. They're all younger bucks who grew up on the reservation, and never tasted the war-path. Of course they were champing at the bit. It didn't take much for Maco and Nachito to strike the spark that made them break."

"Your patrols haven't run down anything?"

The colonel's lips twisted around the cigar. "Ever try chasing an eddy of dust? It flurries up, but the desert swallows it. We've found nothing. This bunch is well-led." He eyed McGivern with a faint irony. "Maco's an old friend of yours, isn't he?"

McGivern shrugged. The enmity between the Apache war chief and the ex-scout went back a long way, to a time when McGivern had guided the troops that had rounded up Maco and some other hostile hot-bloods and returned them to the reservation. Soon Maco had broken out, and in retaliation had gone out of his way to kill McGivern's best friend, a prospecting partner. McGivern had offered his services free to the troops that had brought Maco to bay a second time. Coming to Fort Laughlin to capitulate, Maco had suddenly, in wild fury, attacked

McGivern with a knife, and had been thrown in the post guardhouse for a month.

"This Nachito, though . . . I never heard of him."

"He's a bad one," the colonel said flatly. "Can't tell you much, except in years he's not much past twenty — but already a war chief with four years of experience as Geronimo's lieutenant behind him. That was in Sonora. I expect he came north to get a band of his own. Maco is crazy blind with hatred for all white-eyes, and Nachito must have played on that to get the weight of Maco's prestige among the San Carlo Apaches behind him. This Nachito is clever and dangerous — as you may find out."

McGivern's eyes veiled. "You think so?"

"It's in your mind to trace those gunrunners through the 'Paches, isn't it? You have my blessing. Unofficially, of course."

McGivern didn't reply, but his jaw had hardened. He came slowly to his feet. Watching him, the colonel knew another pang of regret. *Revenge is all he's got now,* he thought. *God forgive me if it destroys him.*

"Mac, you're dead on your feet. Go to my quarters and get some sleep. Make your plans later."

McGivern said tonelessly, "Not much to plan, Dud. When's the funeral?"

"It'll be a mass burial, early tomorrow," the colonel said awkwardly. "If you like —"

"No," McGivern said in the same toneless

way. "The post cemetery will be all right. I'll stay for the burial, then start back to Silver City. I want to wrap up my affairs — first."

The colonel stood at the window, watching McGivern's high, lean figure trudge toward officers' row. It would be a long and danger-geared trail for the ex-scout . . . yet McGivern was the man to take the wild land out there in his two hands and wring what he wanted out of it.

3

Three months later McGivern rode into Saguaro, a ranch-center village two hundred miles west of San Carlos. He was thinned past gauntness now, worn to lean rawhide. He wore his old scout clothes — age-rusty cavalry pants with the yellow stripe down the outseam, a discolored buckskin jacket, and knee-length Apache moccasins with the stiff, upcurling toe. A curl-brimmed smoke-smudged hat that was pulled almost eyebrow level, and a two weeks' growth of neglected black beard, along with the alkali and dried sweat that stained his clothes, gave him a scrubby, raffish appearance. A holstered Colt, buckled over the jacket, sagged at his hip. The Winchester he'd found at the canyon massacre was in the saddle boot under his knee. His untiring quest had long since become ingrained into a cold, watchful pattern on his face.

He knew these things in a detached way, without caring. Jogging now through the residential end of Saguaro, a side street lined with flowered lawns, picket fences, and summer-smoldering rows of poplar, he was concerned only with a silent conviction that the search would end here.

Late afternoon shadows like gaunt fingers

rippled over horse and rider as they turned into the main street. In addition to its saloons and several stores, Saguaro boasted a feed company, a livery stable, a freighting yard, blacksmith and gun shops, and a couple of eating places. Shade trees of oak, ash and sycamore marched along the business district, relieving the usual drab and weathered monotony of a small range town.

McGivern's shuttling glance found and stopped on an aging frame building with the nearly weathered away legend ROOMS across its upper front. He turned in at the tie rail, dismounted, and tied his horse. He uncinched his blanket and saddlebags, lifted them to his shoulder, skirted the rail and tramped onto the narrow porch.

Two men loafed in chairs back-tilted against the building, their booted feet propped on a railing between the porch columns. McGivern halted. The bigger man glanced up at him, smiled disarmingly, and lowered his feet. The other man stared at McGivern without moving. He was young, lath-narrow, with a pinched face. His banjo eyes were reckless and hungry, waiting for trouble, wanting it.

"I don't like stepping over your legs, friend," McGivern said quietly.

"Walk around," the narrow man said, shifting a straw he was chewing to the corner of his thin lips. "There's a whole street to walk in."

"Maybe you better start walking," McGivern said.

The man came swiftly to his feet, hooking a thumb in his gunbelt. He flicked the straw back and forth with his tongue. "You're mouthy, mister. We don't like mouthy strangers."

McGivern felt his muscles pull up with the tension of a week on the trail, of months of obsessive purpose. *Tough, cocky gunslick,* he thought, and then, warningly: *Don't let him rawhide you; you can't afford a fight now.*

He glanced at the big man who was quietly watching this, a faint smile on his lips. He was a great-shouldered fellow with an imperial Roman profile crowned by a tight cluster of golden curls. His eyes were gray and watchful, tolerant eyes that seemed to reserve judgment, with an amused and cynical twinkle in them.

"You know him?" McGivern asked the big man, nodding at the feisty one.

"Guilty," the big man said. He chuckled.

"You know better," McGivern went on thinly. "If the cub wants to cut my sign, tell him to cut it right."

The narrow youth began coldly, "Listen, you out-at-the-pants drifter —"

"Cinch up, Pride," the big man said sharply. "If you want to play with mud pies, there's a whole streetful of ingredients. Step away." Pride did not move; a slow flush darkened his face. "I said step away!"

Pride met McGivern's stare for a long hot moment, then moved back against the wall. McGivern walked by them without a backward

23

glance, shouldered open and stepped through the double doors of the hotel. The lobby was not really cool, but it seemed so after the glaring street. McGivern paused inside, breathing deeply the aroma of frying steaks he could hear crackling in the kitchen. His belly knotted with hunger. He walked on to the desk and asked the young clerk for a room.

"And how long will you be staying, sir?"

"No telling." McGivern signed the register. "What time you serve supper?"

"Oh . . . in fifteen minutes. That'll be two dollars in advance. Room one-oh-four."

McGivern paid, received his key, and tramped up the staircase. He halted in the shadowy corridor at the head of the stairs as the lobby doors creaked open. He watched the two men from the porch come in and cross the lobby. The big man halted by the desk and spoke quietly to the clerk, who turned the register book around. The big man scanned it.

The ghost of a smile touched McGivern's lips. He pivoted on moccasined feet and faded down the corridor to his room.

"Thomas McGivern, Silver City," the big man read aloud from the register. "Mean anything to you, Charlie?"

The clerk yawned. "Sorry, Reggie; never laid eyes on him."

The big man nodded, turned, and walked back to the doorway, trailed by his companion.

24

They stepped out onto the walk.

"How about you?"

"What?"

"Ever see him before?"

Pride scratched his head, scowling. "Naw. Heard that name somewheres . . . McGivern."

Reggie cuffed his battered hat back on his golden curls, frowning at McGivern's horse at the rail. "That's a McClellan saddle. And he was wearing cavalry pants. Doesn't walk or sit his horse like a soldier-boy; still. . . ."

"It could be trouble," Pride put in, his black eyes dancing hotly. "Want me to brace him?"

"No, you fool!" Reggie said sharply. "You'll tip our hand sure. . . ."

"Not if he's dead," Pride said gently.

Reggie gave him a contemptuous glance. "Don't bet on it. This one can handle himself."

"Why'd he back down?"

Reggie shook his head pityingly. "Fella, you never learn. This one's poison. I smell it. Have to feel him out careful, learn why he's here. Strangers with Army gear don't ride in every day, even every month. If his business isn't with us, no point in drawing his attention."

"So what do we do?" Pride asked querulously.

Reggie pulled his lower lip. "I'll see Belden, talk it over. You stay and watch the hotel. If he comes out, follow him. But don't start anything. Hear me, Pride?"

"Sure, sure," Pride said softly.

McGivern unlocked his door and entered. The room was a hot little cubbyhole stale with sealed-off air, furnished with a washstand, a battered dresser and an iron bedstead. He lowered his saddle and gear onto the bed, skirted it to reach the window. He wrestled the warped sash up a couple of inches, letting the hot dusty air of the street wash through the room.

Voices drifted from the sidewalk below, then broke off. McGivern saw the big man move from under the porch awning and angle downstreet, walking fast. He turned into the freight office. McGivern moved back from the window, again smiling faintly. Five minutes in Saguaro, and he'd drawn lightning. He had no wish to keep his identity secret. Deliberately whetting their curiosity might provoke a giveaway move from the enemy, and he was steeled for the risk involved.

His smile faded as he stepped to the washstand, peeling off his jacket and calico shirt. It wasn't enough to be privately certain; he needed proof. For all he knew, he might have to fight the whole town. They couldn't be sure why he was here. While they were unsure, his life would probably not be imperiled. All the same, he decided warily that he'd watch his back if they had more like Pride on their payroll.

He poured water into the cracked basin and sponged off his lanky upper body. He toweled himself slowly, frowning out the window, unconsciously rubbing the long pale scar across his shoulder and upper back where Maco's knife had made its slashing try four years ago. He needed information about the town and its people; he would, he thought wryly, need to know whom he could trust, with no more than shrewd guesswork to go on.

Till now it had been a matter of dogged patience, of ferreting out and tracking down leads. Yet it had consumed time, precious time. Weeks, months of it.

At first he'd thought his best prospects would lay with the Apaches. He knew them and they knew him. After leaving the fort he'd headed back to Silver City and sold out his freighting outfit to one of his competitors. That part of his life was a closed chapter. He had built a position of civic responsibility, given up a life free as the wind because he'd cared for a woman more. Though the reason for that self-denial was gone, in his thoughts the old life was almost as tasteless.

The sale completed, he'd packed his meager belongings and headed north for San Carlos. But he'd found Apache friends with whom he'd drunk and joked strangely reticent, and he knew the tribal grapevine had gone ahead and the tribal ranks had closed against him. He was only another, *pinda-likoye* now, a hated enemy who wanted to learn matters which would hurt their brothers.

At first stymied, McGivern had realized finally

that the solution was so close he'd missed it. Those rifles could only have reached this remote territory by wagon freighters — a business which he knew inside and out. He had written letters, enlisted the help of teamsters and freighter friends.

He'd learned that four hundred Winchesters and forty thousand rounds of .44-.40 ammunition had been shipped from New York by steamer to New Orleans, where they were held in the warehouse of a Frank Belden. This Belden had a brother, George, in Saguaro, Arizona, to whom he freighted supplies overland at cut rates which had enabled George Belden to monopolize the choicest freight contracts in the territory, with the mines, the Army, Indian traders, and cattle towns. And Saguaro, where George Belden made his headquarters, was only a hundred miles from San Carlos Reservation.

Four hundred rifles. Forty thousand shells. That was a lot of death in the wrong hands, McGivern thought soberly as he set out his soap and razor. Colonel Cahill had been right. This was a big thing, touching the lives of every Apache and white in the territory. At least a part of that shipment had already gone into the hands of Maco and Nachito and their band, and their successful maraudings had sent a wave of restiveness throughout Apacheland. Even at this late date, a new full-scale uprising could be in the offing.

How much of the gun shipment had already

passed into Apache hands? This was the question that kept turning in McGivern's mind. Probably the arms were being shipped from New Orleans in gradual amounts, mixed with other freight to avert suspicion. If so, there was still a possibility of catching the gunrunners red-handed, and on this assumption McGivern must set his plans.

He shaved carefully, shrugged into a fairly clean shirt from his warbag, locked his room and went downstairs. He ate supper in the almost empty dining room, lingered over coffee and a cigar, then stood and went leisurely out through the lobby to the front porch.

Dusk was closing down over Saguaro, squares of oily light beginning to fill the windows. McGivern halted on the porch to relight his dead cigar, slowly turning out of a slight wind to face the row of lounging chairs. A single narrow figure slouched there; the matchlight washed against Pride's glinting eyes as he hunched forward a little, letting his feisty stare hit McGivern's.

McGivern snapped the match in his fingers and dropped it. He stepped off the porch and untied his horse. He led it downstreet to the livery stable and left orders for its feed and care with the hostler. Upstreet again, he turned in at the Belle Fourche Casino opposite the hotel. He paused by the swing doors to look back, and saw Pride stand and start across the street. *He'll be watching me tonight*, McGivern thought unconcernedly, and pushed on through the swing doors.

0ᴛ343

The Belle Fourche was good-sized for a small town. The wide, vaulted front room was over-hung with a curling strata of cigar smoke and the smell of stale whisky. The long mahogany bar was well-crowded for a week night. At the back of the room was a wide archway spanned by beaded black curtains, and from beyond these came the rattle of roulette wheels and the murmurs of card players.

McGivern was about to move on to the bar when the broad shape of a woman pushed through the beaded curtains from the gambling room. She halted, hand still raised from parting the curtains, then waddled forward to meet him. "For God's sake — Tom McGivern!"

McGivern couldn't stop his own broad grin, stiff and unaccustomed as it felt. "Ma. Ma Gates."

Ma Gates never changed, McGivern thought, meeting her handclasp. She looked much as she had thirteen years ago when he, a callow, timid boy just off his first trail drive, had seen her in a bawdy house in Abilene. She wasn't fat, despite her thick girth balanced by her unusual height. There were a few more lines, maybe, around the shrewd, pale eyes — eyes wise and tired from viewing three generations of seamy frontier life, from the keelboat days of the Natchez Trace to the raw young Arizona mining towns, and the lines reminded McGivern that she must be past sixty now. Her full, high-necked black gown and lofty forehead under the red-dyed billow of her hair gave her an impressive look, like a kind of tribal sachem, which befitted the living legend she'd become throughout the West.

"For God's sake," Ma said again, still holding his hand as she glanced around. "There's a table, Mac; let's sit down. What's happened to you?"

They sat at a corner table, and Ma Gates signaled the bartender for a bottle of the house's best. "Nothing much," McGivern answered. "Still drifting." He noted that Pride had already bellied to the bar, glowering at him in the back-bar mirror.

Ma leaned her thick arms on the table, facing him, her hard, shrewd eyes narrowed. "Don't lie to me, fella. You've changed. You always was a lad who seen a lot, but it never really got to you before."

McGivern's jaw hardened. He was about to speak when the bartender came with a tray bearing a bottle and two glasses. He poured their drinks and left.

"Forget it," Ma said then, brusquely. "Was curious, that's all. Always fancied you. You was never one of them sugar-mouthed hypocrites who sneaked into a cathouse the back way and otherwise crossed the street to avoid an honest chippie."

McGivern had to grin. "There was never any fooling you, Ma." He looked down at his glass, hardly believing his good luck at finding Ma Gates in Saguaro. She knew more about any

31

place and its people than did the lifelong residents. McGivern hadn't seen her since the city fathers had hustled her and her girls out of Silver City three years ago. Always close-mouthed and no easy mark, she'd open up to one of the few people she fancied.

He glanced around at the Casino and its furnishings. "You're doing all right, it seems. But where's the old line?"

Ma chuckled. "I still hire girls. But only to sing, shill at the tables, talk with the lonesome drinkers. The West is gotten filled up, Mac, settled down. The towns've got banks, schools, churches, and citizens who are solid as all hell. Folks get pious soon as they can afford to be."

McGivern smiled. "And you too?"

Ma Gates shrugged. "Why not? I got to live. At that, even the Belle Fourche is only just tolerated since I took over. Lot of the community pillars remember Ma Gates from the old days." A glint of unpleasant humor touched her eyes. "I could point out a lot of dirty wash on *their* back lines, was I minded."

McGivern laughed. "I'll bet you could, too." He leaned forward. "Look, I wonder if you know —"

"Hell, I know you now."

The harsh voice cut into McGivern's quiet speech, and he looked up. Pride Bloom was coming from the bar toward their table, weaving a little. With a corner of his mind, McGivern had taken note of the three fast whiskies Pride had downed — enough to crowd the gunman to rashness.

Pride halted by their table, glaring down at him. "I 'member," he said. "McGivern. You was scout for Fort Laughlin. You got a friend of mine, Jack Hurdy, sent to the Federal pen."

"Have your drink, Mac," Ma said, not even glancing at Pride. "It's out of my private bottle."

McGivern lifted his glass, let the fiery liquor coast down his throat. It warmed his belly, set his nerves tingling. *All right,* he thought resignedly, *it had to come.*

Pride was left flat-footed and ignored. He glared foolishly. "You listen damnit."

"I knew Mescal Jack," McGivern said steadily. "He was whisky-running to the 'Paches, and I caught him. Sneaking, yellow-backed half-breed. You say he's your friend?"

"Stan' up, you," Pride snarled.

"Look, you snot-nosed troublerouser," Ma began.

"Shut up, Fatty. I'm tellin' Buckskin, here, to stand up."

In dead silence McGivern scraped back his chair and came to his feet.

4

In build they were evenly matched. McGivern, usually heavier, had sloughed every ounce of excess weight in these last months, had pared down to sheer bone and muscle. Pride looked ganglier, almost awkward in his movements, but McGivern had noted on the hotel porch earlier that the man could move with a catlike grace if he chose. Nor did he believe that Pride was as drunk as he appeared; his eyes gleamed warily, unglazed. His elbow-rolled sleeves showed wiry, knotted forearms.

Ma stood now, backing from the table; at the same time Pride moved in, feinting at McGivern's midriff with his left hand, then throwing a straight arm at his face. It was a fast, neat combination; McGivern barely turned his head in time, then rolled back a pace with the blow so that Pride's fist glanced lightly off his cheekbone and spent its momentum in the lunge he couldn't stop. As he stumbled against the ex-scout, McGivern lifted his shoulder against Pride's chin with an impact that clicked his jaws together. McGivern whipped his right hand up and down, chopping the edge of his rock-hard lower palm against Pride's neck. He jerked Pride's gun from its holster and tossed it to a bystander, then caught Pride by the neck and threw him roughly away. Pride was flung on his back across the table, which skittered away under his weight, crashing him to the floor.

McGivern stepped to the chair he'd just vacated and put his hands on its back, waiting. Pride came up on his hands and knees, shaking his head like a ringy bull. He came upright suddenly, legs driving against the floor, diving low at McGivern before he was fully on his feet. McGivern dropped the chair on its side and kicked it, shooting it in front of Pride's legs, which plunged between the rungs and tripped him. His face plowed against the splintery floor.

A riffle of laughter came from the tense bystanders, and McGivern guessed that more than one of them had been mauled by this bully-boy. But McGivern had received his own maulings at the hands of Apache bucks in reservation games, warriors trained from youth to every trick of rough-and-tumble wrestling. Twice he could have followed through and battered Pride senseless; cold patience checked him.

Pride climbed to his feet, slowly this time, drawing the back of his hand across his bleeding mouth and nose. He rushed, and McGivern met him with a savage impact, bringing up the heel of his hand in a vicious clout to Pride's chin. The gunman's head snapped back, but not before he'd wrapped his arm about McGivern's neck in a crude headlock. McGivern kept his body bent, away from the lift of knee or boot which Pride tried to bring up. His face mashed against Pride's rank-smelling shirt, he concentrated on throwing wicked, jolting punches to Pride's middle. The gunnie's ability to absorb punishment, yet hang doggedly to his hold, was impressive. He groaned with each pummeling blow, unable to crush McGivern's corded neck muscles with his armhold, but he wouldn't let go.

McGivern knew with a growing baffled anger that to free himself he'd have to reverse the headlock with a counterlock on Pride. He worked to wedge his hand in from behind through the choking circle of Pride's arm, then brought it up at the back of the man's neck. He had his grip now — a half nelson that brought him behind Pride. Then he twisted savagely, breaking the necklock and whipping his free hand under Pride's opposite arm. He clamped both hands at the back of Pride's neck in a deadly full nelson with which he might easily break the man's neck.

Their struggling had carried them almost against the bar, which the customers had vacated for a wide space. The fighters were facing the bar now, and McGivern relentlessly bent Pride's head downward till his face almost touched his knees. Then he suddenly released Pride with a vicious shove. Pride stumbled once, bringing his head up to catch his balance, and the edge of the bar caught him full in the face with a sickening sound. His knees folded;

he sagged against the bar and then toppled on his back, his bleeding face turned up.

McGivern stood above him, breathing gustily. The flurry of talk lifted excitedly around him, and as swiftly hushed when the batwing doors creaked open. The big blond man he'd seen earlier with Pride stood there. He advanced into the room, watching McGivern curiously. Halting by Pride, he prodded the motionless form with a speculative toe, then turned his sleepy gaze back on McGivern.

"Get Pride out of here, Reggie," Ma Gates said sharply. "And tell Belden he'll be gettin' a bill for damages . . . Call it moral damage," she added with vindictive satisfaction.

"All right," Reggie said without glancing at her. He smiled with no censure at McGivern. "I know he bought that, but I think you broke his nose."

"I meant to," McGivern said gently.

Reggie's eyes narrowed; his grin stayed neutral. "Don't get snakey, friend. No sweat of mine." On the floor, Pride groaned. Reggie bent and hauled him effortlessly to his feet, saying, "Come on, you damned fool."

He started toward the door, supporting Pride, and halted there as a man came in, confronting them. "What happened, Harlan?"

Reggie jerked his head over his shoulder at McGivern, said curtly, "Ask him," and pushed on past, the swing doors closing behind him.

The newcomer was McGivern's age. His

stocky body was clad in a spotless white shirt and black trousers stuffed in high-polished jack-boots. A flat-crowned black Stetson rode his sandy hair without crease or flourish. A sheriff's star shone on his neatly-buttoned black vest. His long face had a no-nonsense, businesslike set that went with his suit, but somehow McGivern wasn't impressed.

He surveyed McGivern coldly. "Did you hit him?"

"As hard as I could."

Ma chuckled. The sheriff looked at her, the distaste deepening in his face. "I've warned you about trouble, Mrs. Gates."

"Come off your high horse with me, Pauly-boy," Ma said dryly.

The sheriff flushed as though her words, her tone, had touched a raw nerve. "I'm trying to do my duty," he said stiffly. "You make it difficult."

"Duty's a high-soundin' word," Ma said imperturbably, "but that ain't what makes you tick, sonny. It used to be booze, now it's Belden."

Somebody laughed. The sheriff swung his glare at the man, then at McGivern. "We don't need your kind in Saguaro, saddle bum."

"You want to move me?" McGivern asked softly.

The sheriff dropped his hand to his gun, but that was all. There was a general hoot of laughter from the crowd. His face burning; the lawman turned on his heel and walked out.

Ma touched McGivern's arm. "Let's sit, Mac. Where was we?"

McGivern righted their table and chairs, and when they were seated he said: "We were talking about people. Like your sheriff."

Ma snorted disgustedly. "Paul Hornbeck. He was the town drunk before George Belden decided he needed a sheriff who'd burp every time George swallowed. He took Paul out of the gutter, dressed him up, paid for his campaign, and bullied and barbecued a majority of the voters in his favor. Nobody wants trouble with Belden. Paul took it serious, straightened up, quit the bottle, settled down to work. That means lettin' Belden's bullies, like Pride Bloom, raise all hell, while soft-pedaling complaints anyone has about George Belden and his business ethics. Paul ain't bad, just gutless. Feel kind of sorry for the pompous ninny. . . ."

"This Belden. He the power in Saguaro?"

Ma eyed him thoughtfully. "Paul maybe gave you some good advice, Mac."

"About moving on?"

"You beat up Belden's testiest bully. Belden owns the freight company, half the stores, the hotel, the stable, two of the three saloons. I've kept the Belle Fourche going only because I know how to give better entertainment than any of his places, though he's had his barkeeps cut liquor prices, even operate at a loss, to try and break me." Ma's wise old eyes narrowed. "Belden's a new kind of crook, Mac; he operates behind the sanction of the respectable element. The banker, the merchants, the town council, all know Saguaro is dependent on his business enterprises, and they'll close their eyes to a lot. Like when a rival freight yard tries to start, only to have their teamsters shot up, their wagons burned — by 'unknown' riders. Like when Belden's tough nuts insult their wives and daughters on the streets —"

"The big fellow," McGivern interrupted. "Reggie. Who's he?"

"Reggie Harlan. Sort of a right-hand troubleshooter for Belden. Does all the legwork. His front is managin' Belden's Chain Anchor spread — ten miles east of town. It used to be a fine ranch till Belden came to Saguaro two years ago and bought it. Rumor has it he was one of that New York Tweed Ring. He talks and acts Eastern, an' he's got plenty of crooked political and business savvy. Anyways, he's made the Chain Anchor over into a general headquarters for all his activities. It's a big spread, with no one around for miles to get in his way. He runs a few cattle for a blind, but there's not an honest puncher on the place. His whole crew of tough nuts and hired guns hang out there, with Reggie Harlan to keep 'em in line."

"You figure I'm in trouble with this crowd already?" McGivern murmured.

Ma Gates grinned shrewdly. "Depends," she said, "on why you're here. You was settled down in Silver City with a payin' freight business, last

40

I seen you. Your stomping days were over. But here you are, a ragtag-an'-bobtail drifter miles from home. You'd be here for a reason — and the reason just might concern George Belden, as he's the only thing hereabouts big enough to bother with. Aside from the fact that Pride Bloom is a grudge-holdin' skunk and you'd best sport an extra eye in the back of your head, George'll just naturally stomp you if he finds you in his way."

McGivern smiled at her perception, but said lazily, "Maybe I came out of my way to see an old friend."

"Hell, I saw your face when you saw me. You was surprised." Ma swung her hefty bulk up from the chair. "I got to check on the gamblin' room. Don't go away; I'll be back. I'll send you company, meantime."

"Don't bother," McGivern said quickly, but Ma was already moving back to the gambling room at her heavy, rolling walk. A minute later a girl came through the beaded curtains and over to McGivern's table.

"May I sit down?" Her voice was low, musical.

He didn't want to talk to this or any girl, pleasant as she might be, but it was Ma's gesture for old time's sake, he knew. He only nodded, yet an impulse made him stand quickly as the girl drew the chair out and wait till she was seated.

She regarded him intently, curiously, and he returned the look. She was tall, willow slim,

41

with clear gray eyes widely set in a slimly molded face. Her hair was arranged in a high coif that caught the tawdry lampglow as a blaze of white gold. She was young and strikingly attractive, this alone setting her apart from the usual percentage girl. But it wasn't that which prompted his curiosity. An indefinable air of well-bred dignity touched her voice, her carriage and movements. Even the knee-length gown that bared her arms and shoulders was simple, unspangled, ungarish, though of a rich material.

"Are you a friend of Mrs. Gates, Mr. McGivern?" she asked. He noted now the crisp New England accent of her words — affected-sounding to the Western ear, but somehow admirable with the low, pleasing modulation of her voice.

"Yes'm. Will you have a drink?"

"No, thank you. They call me Georgette."

He glanced up, startled. "That's —" He bit the sentence off, wondering what had prompted it. Few things should surprise him any more.

She nodded calmly, but a faint brittleness edged her words. "Yes, it is a bawd's name. Not my real one, of course, but still not inappropriate. There are many ways of prostituting one's self."

McGivern felt his face burn. He couldn't reconcile the well-bred, quiet restraint of this girl's manner with her unconcerned candor, nor was he certain of the meaning of her enigmatic words. "I didn't mean —"

"It hardly matters. However, I happen to be a singer. The Silver Thrush of the Belle Fourche. Mrs. Gates has tempered the otherwise tawdry title by playing up what she calls my natural 'class' . . . the idea being that the customers get a forbidden thrill out of watching and hearing a lady-apparent with high-toned airs singing inelegant ballads. If these airs puzzle you, consider them part of the act. I deliberately project 'class' — or its illusion. Often there's little difference, don't you think?"

He stirred uncomfortably. "I wouldn't know."

She eyed him with measuring candor. "You don't look as though you'd know, either. Especially after I saw you rough up that man. But why did Mrs. Gates ask me to sit with you? Why not one of the other girls? Rough-looking customers are quite uneasy with me — while they appreciate me when they're part of a mob."

The brittleness had mounted in her voice, and he felt an inward stir of protest. "I liked your voice before."

"Has it changed?" She sounded startled.

"It has. It's cold, harsh."

Her clear eyes took a fresh measure of him. "You notice things, don't you?"

"That's my business. Or was. Army scout."

She smiled suddenly, erasing the bitter harshness that had settled around her mouth. "I've seen Army scouts before. But none that —"

"I beg your pardon."

43

The man spoke stiffly, quietly; McGivern was surprised and mildly annoyed that talking to this girl had relaxed his usual alertness to where he hadn't seen the man approach.

"Good evening, Clyde," the girl said. "Mr. McGivern, this is Mr. Prentiss."

Prentiss extended a soft hand, murmured something, and looked back at the girl. He was about thirty, balding, not over five and a half feet in height. He wore a cheap, neat suit of dark material and his celluloid collar dug high and stiff against his chin. There was something prim and cloistered about him, like any bookish clerk who had worked a lifetime for bigger men and endured a thousand small indignities without complaint.

"Would you care to go for a ride after I finish work tomorrow afternoon, Julia?" Prentiss asked. He glanced nervously over his shoulder, plainly ill at ease in this smoke-filled din of drink and gambling.

"Yes, of course, Clyde," she said, faint irritation in her words. At the man's prissiness, McGivern guessed; he almost smiled at the incongruity of such a man courting a casino girl, and idly wondered about that.

McGivern looked at the girl and was about to speak when Ma Gates bustled back. "All right, honey, back to your stand."

The girl stood, saying quietly, "Perhaps you'll come to hear me sing soon, Mr. McGivern. I can't promise you'll like the fare —"

44

"He'll like it, honey," Ma Gates said sharply, waving a plump hand in dismissal.

McGivern had stood when the girl rose to leave; as she turned back into the gambling hall, he sat down, facing Ma, who leaned her heavy, black-clad arms on the table. "You like Georgette?"

He nodded.

"Figured you would. I remembered how you like 'em — quiet and smart. She's different from the other girls. Reads books, poetry, toney magazines."

"Who's Clyde Prentiss?"

Ma's thin lips twitched. "Bookkeeper over at Belden's Freight Company. Maybe her and him's got something in common, at that. Georgette's real name is Julia Lanphere, and she's from Boston. One of them Beacon Hill swells. Something happened to her back East. Dunno what, and I never asked." Ma showed her thin old harridan's grin. "You could take her away from that mouse, was you minded."

"I'm not."

Ma Gates' snort was eloquent. "Look, this is an old Ma you're talking to — remember?"

"I ran out of wild oats a long time ago, Ma."

"The hell. What are you now — thirty-four, five?" She paused, her wise eyes thoughtful. "You *have* changed, Mac. It shows around your eyes and mouth. It's sort of mean."

"I'll see you tomorrow, Ma," McGivern said quietly. He stood, clamped on his hat, and walked out.

On the boardwalk he paused, breathing the fragrant darkness, mentally checking what he'd learned. George Belden was his man, no doubt of that. He was aware now of a marrow-deep tiredness, and he started across to the hotel. Tomorrow he'd begin the tough job of marshaling evidence, and sleeping on his plans had always been a help. He wondered if Pride's choosing him out had been arranged, and he decided not; still, he'd better move carefully. . . .

5

The morning sun had already touched the clap-boarded fronts of Saguaro's main street from a mellow softness to a brassy glare as Reggie Harlan turned onto the street and headed down toward the freighting yard at its south end. As he drew abreast of the little millinery store, Reggie glanced at Melissa Belden's rig pulled up in front. He had seen her leaving Chain Anchor earlier and now he idly wondered at her frequent trips to town. The ranch cook brought out all the supplies they needed, and Lissa already had enough clothes to outfit a regiment of dowagers. Likely it was boredom that drove her to town, if only to make a few trivial purchases.

Still looking toward the shop, Reggie saw Melissa come out, swinging a hatbox in her hand. Beside her walked Sheriff Paul Hornbeck, carrying two more boxes. Lissa was handsome as always in a gray riding habit, a pert straw hat on the shining auburn coils of her hair, but her face, usually cold and withdrawn as a pale cameo, was faintly flushed as she smiled up at Hornbeck. Both of them saw Reggie then, and Melissa's smile vanished. Harlan lifted his hat, an ironic grin on his wide lips. Hornbeck quickly dropped the purchases in the buckboard, touched his hat to Lissa and walked away.

Reggie rode on, whistling under his breath. Belden's spendthrift wife and Belden's ex-drunk of a sheriff. He almost laughed aloud, wondering if the Old Man knew about this. It looked innocent enough, nothing you could pin down; but Lissa had never blushed, never smiled, for any man, her husband included, in the three years Reggie had worked for Belden.

Harlan's thoughts veered as he passed the hotel veranda and saw a tall, spare man slacked in one of the chairs, watching the currents of life along the main street. So McGivern hadn't ridden on; he was staying over, and the possibilities this suggested were disturbing. Reggie gave the man a neutral nod as he passed, and McGivern nodded back impassively.

Belden's Freighting Company was at street's end. A narrow frame building fronted the street, with the company's name painted across its weathered upper front. A high board fence with an arched entrance began here and ran on for many yards, enclosing the building and off to the right the big wagon yard with its labyrinth of barns and sheds and corrals. Reggie rode through the archway and tied his horse at the rail just off the drive. He mounted the steps leading to the front office.

Halting in the doorway, a fresh amusement deepened in his face as he saw Clyde Prentiss at his high desk and stool. Prentiss was in his shirt-sleeves, his narrow shoulders hunched over his ledgers.

"Hello, Clyde," Reggie said loudly. "How's the girl friend?"

Prentiss looked up, quick dislike pinching his face. Since the prim bookkeeper had started to court a honkytonk girl, Reggie's occasional baitings had become a daily ritual. "Quite well, thank you."

Reggie winked slyly. "Always wondered how she was. Damned if I thought you'd find out, though."

Prentiss' thin fist knotted around his pen and he flushed with anger, but his eyes fell from Reggie's hard, merry gaze. Harlan laughed, clapped him on the shoulder, said lazily, "Attaboy, Clyde, up and at 'em," and walked to the inner office. Beyond this was a short hallway with another door at the end, and from here he walked unannounced into Belden's office.

The inner office was a shabby cubbyhole with a high, grubby window facing the street and another opening on the back lot. The only furniture besides the battered iron filing cabinet in one corner was a roll-top desk with a swivel chair, and a straight-backed visitor's chair. The swivel chair creaked dangerously as its occupant ponderously turned to face the door.

George Belden was a gross tub of a man who must have scaled over three hundred pounds of immense trunk set on short, stocky legs. The best tailor could not have altered his baggy black suit to fit his grotesque form. His keglike thighs almost split his trousers. His belt vanished in his belly under a shocking expanse of yellow-and-green-checked waistcoat. His features were incongruously small and delicate in his egg-bald head with its gray fringing of hair. He might once have been handsome in a cold, incisive way before his lower face became swallowed in its bulging wattles.

"Good morning, Reggie," he wheezed, "and close the window before you sit down. The draft stimulates my arthritis."

He wouldn't breathe if he didn't have me to blow his nose, Reggie thought, stepping to the window and slamming down the sash. He toed the visitor's chair around and sank into it, cuffing his hat back on his head. He took a straw from his pocket and chewed it, thoughtfully eyeing Belden.

"Saw your wife this morning."

Belden cocked a brow over one fish-cold eye. "At the ranch, of course."

"There, and in town. Your boozehead sheriff was carrying her packages."

"Ha ha ha," Belden said. He didn't laugh; he said it. Belden never laughed. "If fair Lissa and pious Paul find mutual pleasure in a tête-à-tête, why not? Swine who are content to rut are less likely to gore the stykeeper. And I keep a full sty, don't you agree, Reginald?"

Reggie stared at the fat man through half-veiled eyes, silently hating him. George Belden, he had long since discovered, had no emotional direction at all except his ruthless ambition, toward which all legitimate or crooked activities were aimed. Even Reggie, with his own comfortably slack ethics, caviled at this contemptuous, ice-like indifference to humanity.

Reggie Harlan, scion of one of New York's oldest families, had been kicked out of a half-dozen excellent schools for as many raw escapades, until his father had disowned him completely. Afterward he'd drifted slowly West, going from drinking and wenching to stealing, gun brawls, and worse. He had no regrets, because he had no more ambition at thirty than he'd had at twenty. He did have an intense and energetic love of life, and luxuriated in his small and large vices; whereas Belden was dominated by single-minded greed that ruled out everything else.

"Consider," Belden murmured now. "Lissa's assets of beauty and background will someday be useful to a man who is going places, perhaps to the governor's chair. I can't afford to have her run off because of discontent."

"She might just," Reggie said softly, "run off with Hornbeck."

"Ha ha ha," Belden said, his wattles shaking. "Lissa's first love is the clothes, money, and luxury which *I* provide. Hornbeck, that worm? The only thing holding him from the bottle is a slender thread of respectability — which *I* gave him. Let them have their rosy little affair." He switched subjects without changing the reedy

51

tonelessness of his voice. "Nachito is to make contact with the ranch today. Why aren't you out there?"

"I came to find out if the last shipment of guns came in this morning. Our deal with the 'Paches is for two hundred rifles, like before."

Belden scowled. "The wagons haven't arrived yet, and they were due yesterday. It's a long overland haul; they could have gotten tied up at a river crossing, stalled in mud, anything. We have one hundred and fifty rifles and fifteen thousand rounds ready for Nachito. Can't you promise him the rest?"

Harlan smiled thinly. "Look, I've done all our business with that Apache; you ain't met him. He's a businessman and politician in a breech-clout. He has to dicker through us, but that don't mean he trusts us farther'n a grasshopper can spit."

"Wise redskin," Belden wheezed sarcastically. "You'll tell him to come again in a week, exactly."

Reggie nodded and started to rise, then hesitated. "That McGivern's still around. Saw him as I rode in."

Belden shifted his elephantine bulk, and the chair shrieked. "You really think he's dangerous?"

"You saw Pride last night after McGivern finished with him," Reggie said flatly. "Pride's dumb, but he's a tough customer. McGivern wasn't even marked."

52

Belden nodded broodingly. "Then, Pride did tell us McGivern was a scout at Fort Laughlin — when he caught that whisky-running pal of Pride's. But that was six years ago. Still, it wouldn't hurt to check on McGivern's movements. Send two of the men in to see me when you get back to the ranch. They'll tail him."

Reggie smiled sardonically. He'd noted McGivern's watchfulness; the man wouldn't be fooled. But this was the best that could be done. "Don't reckon you want me to send Pride?"

"Of course not," Belden snapped. "Keep that hothead out at the ranch from now on. After the way he jumped McGivern, contrary to your orders. . . ."

"I can give him his walking papers."

"No." Belden pursed his thin lips. "Once free of our outfit, the fool would likely brace McGivern. There must be no trouble till we're sure of McGivern — who he is, his purpose here. If he *is* working for the Army, as you surmised, his death would fasten suspicion on us for certain. If it has to come to that, we'll remove him carefully . . ." He paused, steepling his pudgy fingers. "Maybe you'd better tell Nachito to come back in three days. Those rifles are the only proof of our activity, and the sooner we get them off our hands the better . . . with McGivern around. The rest of the arms should be here then. Meanwhile, have a guard posted over the guns we have. Post it day and night."

"All right."

Belden nodded dismissal and Reggie rose and tramped out thoughtfully. He went through the inner office so preoccupied he forgot to bait Clyde in passing. Pausing at the outer office door, he leaned against the jamb and built one of the Mexican cigarettes he favored, letting his gaze move absently over the wagon yard.

Abruptly his hands stilled around the makings; his eyes snapped to focus on the tall form of McGivern. The man was conversing with one of the teamsters over by the corral. As Reggie watched, they shook hands, then McGivern turned and walked back to the archway to leave.

Reggie took a step backward, cutting him from McGivern's view. When he'd looked out cautiously and seen that McGivern was gone, he leisurely finished shaping his twirly and went down the steps. He crossed the wagon yard to the teamster, who had a wagon up on blocks with the wheels off and was greasing the hubs. He said, "Morning, Lafe."

Lafe Elberg returned the greeting and straightened from his job with a grin, wiping his hands on a rag. He was a tough banty of a man whose face was sun-boiled a darker red than his flame-colored whiskers.

"That this McGivern fellow you were talking to?" Harlan asked idly. "The one who massacred Pride?"

Lafe's was the grin of a born brawler. "That's him. I used to work for him."

"Oh?" Reggie casually bent his head, cupped

54

his hands to light his cigarette. "Doesn't look much like a freighting man."

"Hell, yes; got a big outfit in Silver City."

Face expressionless, Reggie waved the match out. "And he wanted to talk over old times?"

"Oh, he ast some questions . . . you know, shop talk."

"About the goods we freight, markets, routes, stuff like that, eh?"

Reggie felt a nudge of surprise when Lafe answered, "Nope. Wanted to know about the men working here, said he might be expanding business and be needin' more teamsters. Our bunch is nothing but the best, and I told him so."

Harlan smiled. "Hope we won't be losing you, Lafe."

"Not a chance; Mr. Belden pays the most and treats you the best."

Always provided you keep on his side, Reggie thought dryly. He switched the subject, exchanged a few moments of small talk with Lafe, then said good-bye and walked back to his horse. He mounted and turned the animal, riding as far as the archway.

Here Harlan halted, glancing up and down the street, his attention sharp. Exactly what McGivern had been digging for mystified him, but he felt uneasily sure that the man's questioning of Lafe had been no idle whim.

In a moment he saw McGivern ride from the livery barn a block down and turn his horse west from town. When McGivern had swung out of sight, Reggie nudged his mount forward, his face grim. McGivern was taking the wagon road that connected Chain Anchor with town. Any stable boy could have told him the way to Belden's ranch . . . but what, if McGivern knew, had triggered his certainty?

6

He'd been lucky, McGivern reflected as he jogged his sorrel past the last house. His first re-action at the sight of Belden's sprawling wagon yard had been a fatalistic despair. The guns could be cached anywhere in that maze of sheds. Then he had spotted Lafe, a former man of his, and a few questions had convinced him there were no illegal caches in the yard. The men who worked Belden's Freighting Company were rough, bluff and honest, like Lafe himself. McGivern hadn't risked further querying, but he knew that gunrunners would not store hun-dreds of rifles under the noses of honest men. The Winchester '73's were in big demand, dis-tributed for sale as fast as they were freighted into an area, and large numbers in storage would certainly smell amiss; the gunrunner was a breed despised and hated everywhere.

It was only logical that once the guns had reached Saguaro they had passed into the care of those who would see them safely into the eager hands of Apache renegades. Ma Gates had said that Belden's big ranch ten miles east of town was his real headquarters, stocked with toughs and gunnies, and it was only good sense to carry on liaison with the Apaches from an isolated ranch rather than from town. The guns could be taken to the ranch a few at a time, concealed in the usual ranch supplies.

McGivern knew that it could prove more difficult to locate a rifle cache there than at the freight yard; a stranger might be shot on sight, and no one the wiser. For now, he just wanted to size up the layout of Chain Anchor. Then he would lay his plans. He gave brief thought to Reggie Harlan, whom he'd noticed watching him from the office as he spoke to Lafe; Harlan had ducked back, but not fast enough. He would question Lafe, of course, and Lafe could only tell him that McGivern was a Silver City freighter looking for men. That would baffle Harlan and his boss still more, McGivern thought with satisfaction.

As he rode, McGivern's preoccupation did not dull his alert senses. Small things — the twirling trail of a rattler which had crossed the road an hour ago, the wagon ruts and Harlan's horsetracks that had been made since, the distant speck of a vulture hovering on static wings over something below, the thud of his mount's hoofs in the heavy dust of the road, betraying the time since the last rain — these were catalogued in the back of his mind and analyzed meaningfully. The terrain was not flat. The road took its way over humpy dunes, skirted lava outcrops. Because his vision was limited here, McGivern's other senses sharpened.

A single sound at his back, a sound not coupled with ordinary desert noises, made him pull up sharply. He slid from his saddle with a fluid twist of his body, Indian-fashion. He knelt and laid his ear to the road. He knew then that a rider was deliberately pacing him at perhaps a hundred yards' distance. He was being followed.

He led his sorrel off the road, circling a broad, flat-topped outcrop split by a great crevice. He guided his horse into the crevice, then took a running jump and landed lightly atop it. He lowered himself on his belly and took off his hat. From here he had an uninterrupted view of the road, though few white men could have detected his hiding place or where he'd left the road.

He was able to pick out the man's approach long before he rode into sight over a rise. It was Reggie Harlan. *Followed me, all right,* McGivern thought with a silent token of respect: Harlan had had his number from the start, and after speaking to Lafe, he had an inkling of what McGivern had in mind.

When the big man had passed out of view beyond a dune, McGivern slid off the rock. He mounted and reined the sorrel around; he could not follow the road to Chain Anchor now. Harlan, forewarned, would see that he didn't get within a half mile of the place by road. That meant he'd have to circle wide and come up from the north or south. It would take time, with his ignorance of this rugged terrain, Mc-

Givern knew resignedly. But he had to assess the ranch layout by daylight before he could lay a definite plan. . . .

He began a broad swing to the north. After a half hour of steady traveling, the land ironed out and flattened away to the north and east. He carefully gauged the illusive, heat-dancing distances. The ranch was ten miles east of town, and he'd come a good two miles from town before leaving the road. He would head due east for eight miles, then turn south to hit the ranch.

The land held its flat, hard-baked appearance as he ate up the remaining miles, with the sun hot against his right side, then swung south by instinct. Ahead now a sandstone-and-shale hogback ridge gleamed crimson. He slowed, frowning. The ridge was a good hundred feet high, with steep walls insurmountable by a horseman, and it cut directly across his path for miles, as far as he could see. Then he made out where a canyon deeply scored the rimrock, as though a giant wedge had been driven from top to base. Coming nearer, he cut sign on wheel ruts leading into the canyon mouth. That meant that the V-cleft made a handy route which pierced to the hogback's opposite side. The tracks had been made by a heavily weighted vehicle; he considered that thoughtfully.

He put his horse directly into the canyon — and halted almost at once. He dismounted, eyes fixed on horsetracks tramped into the soft, sandy floor. They were fresh, yet not cleanly etched. He stooped and touched them, feeling a cold sensation along his spine. These tracks had been made only a few minutes ago — by a horse neither barefoot nor iron-shod. The hoofs had been bound up in thin, tough hides; and he knew that only Chiricahua Apaches muffled their ponies' hoofs with deerhide stockings.

He mounted and made his way cautiously up the canyon. A heavy rubble of shale chunks, dislodged from above, littered the floor. McGivern couldn't keep his sorrel's hoofs from clipping an occasional rock with small tinny echoes that made him wince. If the Apache rider was only minutes ahead, he'd surely pick up the sound.

McGivern's eyes were ceaselessly ferreting out the trail, and just short of a sharp bend in the canyon ahead he saw a change in the Apache pony's steady lope. The rider had briefly halted and then the tracks continued, deep-dug and hurried. *Stopped when he heard my horse, then he kicked it up,* McGivern thought. He spurred his own animal, but came to an abrupt halt before he reached the narrow-angled turn. The pony's imprints continued, but the sudden lessening of weight was perceptible.

He left his horse, but it kept going, McGivern thought in brief puzzlement. Where had the man gone? Then he understood. Crowded against the inner turn was a lava buttress about head high to a standing man. The Apache had quirted his pony hard, at the same time springing from its back onto the buttress. There was the faint scraping of loose stone atop the buttress, where he'd landed on his feet. Then he'd proceeded to scale the almost vertical wall like a cat, taking advantage of every hold. Now he was out of sight somewhere high on the talus just beyond the turn, balled in a crouch on one of the protruding shale ledges that laced the upper gorge.

McGivern considered these things in the flash of a second — and also that the Apache thought he had to deal with a sense-dulled white-eyes. Nor would a white man look for an enemy high on these walls — unless he knew that conditioning to dizzy heights was part of the Apache puberty-ritual test. This one's agility proved his youth.

McGivern soundlessly released a held breath. The sharp-eared brave would be suspicious of his sudden halt . . . he kicked his animal into motion and swerved around the turn, his eyes instantly whipping up to scan the rugged cliffside. Yet it came swiftly, instantly, before he had even a glimpse of his enemy.

An arrow breathed past his ear. He flung himself from the saddle, a second arrow grazing his jacket even as he leaped off. He rolled to break his fall on the soft earth, and was for a moment sheltered by the sorrel's body. He scrambled up, made a short crouching run that carried him back to the lava buttress. He dived behind its cover as a third shaft drove into the rock a foot above his back. The quartz tip, splintering, pockmarked his jacket.

He drew his pistol and edged his face around the buttress till he could see the whole wall. Then he saw the blued tip of a rifle barrel nudged over the rim of a shale ledge tilting a good twenty feet above the gorge floor. It had been a matter of pride with the buck to strike first at a lone white man with primitive bow and arrows; these had failed.

McGivern deliberately exposed his shoulder and arm, extending his pistol at arm's length as he fired. Chips flew from the ledge. Suddenly the Apache sprang to his feet, teased into view by his enemy's exposure; he threw his rifle to his shoulder and fired as quick as thought, then immediately dropped prone again.

McGivern felt the slug fan his temple; he yelled and fell backward, out of sight. He rolled on his belly, his gun drawn up by his head and ready. Face pressed to the hot sand, he waited. He heard the Apache's eager descent of the talus, his moccasins clattering down a few shale fragments. With a thud the Indian landed lithely on the sand. He paced slowly forward, warily circling the buttress into McGivern's field of vision. McGivern watched through slitted lids. The Apache was holding the rifle steady, to finish the white man at a twitch of movement.

McGivern's movement was no more than the upflick of his fist that held the cocked .45; he fired point blank from the ground. The Apache's rifle thundered in his hands, but it was pure reflex. The bullet ricocheted down-canyon. McGivern's heavy slug spun him like a rag doll and hammered him in a twisting fall.

McGivern got to his feet and tramped to the fallen man, the .45 still pointed. He placed his foot on the naked shoulder and shoved, turning the youth on his back. The rifle rolled from his limp hands. McGivern stooped and picked it up. The Winchester repeater was still new, but it had seen use. The stock was scratched, the barrel rubbed with vegetable matter to dull the glint.

For a long moment McGivern looked down at the Apache. He was unconscious, his breathing hoarse; blood welled a fiery pattern across the coppery torso from a hole high on the left side. He wasn't over twenty-one, clean-limbed as a young stallion. His was not the usual flat, broad Apache face; it was aquiline and boyish, spanned by a broad band of vermilion paint, with stripes of blue above and below. He wore only a breechclout, a warband to confine his straight black hair, and hip-length moccasins folded down at the knees.

A real old-time broncho Apache, McGivern thought grimly. His hand tightened on the still-leveled pistol. *Why not?* The Winchester was like a cold, hard indictment against his palm. This buck might have been at Creagh Canyon that day . . . *he might have done it.*

The thought beat against McGivern's brain like an angry pulse. His finger made a beginning

64

pressure on the trigger, and as slowly relaxed. This was only a boy, wounded and helpless; the finer sensibilities of a civilized upbringing held his hand. It was the folly and stupid greed of white men that had set off the massacre; the Apaches were fighting for existence itself. Finally there was the cold practical knowledge that this buck had been heading for Chain Anchor, probably a lone agent to arrange for the next liaison of guns. McGivern knew well that force, or its threat, would get nothing out of an Apache; still, an Apache might be wiled out of valuable information by one who knew his language and his people.

With this settled in his mind, McGivern's actions became swift and decisive. He dug a none-too-clean spare shirt from his saddlebag and tore it into strips. He knelt by the unconscious boy and raised him to a sitting position against his knee, finding that the bullet had ranged between his short ribs and gone clear through. Both wounds were bleeding cleanly. McGivern fashioned a makeshift wraparound bandage.

Afterward he walked downcanyon till he found the Indian pony grazing in a grassy pocket. It caught the white man's smell, flattened its ears and sidled away. McGivern spoke a few gutteral Apache words, and the pony — evidently a favorite of its brave — became motionless, and he picked up the trailing reins. Leading it back, he hoisted the body of its master onto it and with his lariat tied the boy's feet together beneath the pony's barrel. Mounting the sorrel, he led the pony to the canyon mouth. There he dismounted and went back on foot to erase the signs of the struggle, systematically brushing out tracks back to the canyon mouth.

Mounted again, he struck eastward, hugging the base of the ridge, where air currents would shift the sands and erase their trail. He restlessly scanned the crumbling, broken surface of the cliff till he located a thirty-foot-high ledge, almost inaccessible. He swung stiffly down, ground-haltered the horses and picked out his route from the ground. Then he began to climb, moccasined toeholds bringing him swiftly to the ledge. Past its rim he saw a shallow cave eroded into the cliffs. This was ideal; it would provide both shade and concealment.

Packing up the brave's limp weight was the hardest part; the third ascent, with saddlebags slung from his shoulder, was easy, but he was exhausted when he rolled onto the ledge. He lay on his back sucking deep breaths, drenched with sweat. Then he crawled on hands and knees into the cave, and knelt by the brave where he had stretched him on his side. He unbound the blood-stiffened bandages and washed the wounds with water from his canteen. They had almost ceased bleeding, and the Apache's rugged constitution would finish the cure. The buck would not travel for a while, though; and he was still unconscious, evidently in shock.

McGivern made a compress and a fresh bandage. Then, as he lifted his canteen to drink, the Apache suddenly spoke. "The first arrow was badly feathered, or you would be dead, white-eyed son of a coyote."

He lowered the canteen, seeing the black eyes glinting with mockery in the gloom. How had the buck known that his captor understood Apache? Then he realized that the boy had spoken only to convey a cold contempt by his tone. Yet he was surprised, it was the way of an Apache prisoner to remain sullenly taciturn.

McGivern answered then, speaking casually: "Did your blind grandmother feather it, boy?"

Only a faint flicker of eyelids betrayed the buck's surprise. Then: "How is it that a white-eyes speaks the tongue of the *Shis-in-day* like one born to it?"

"I have lived at San Carlos. Also I guided the pony soldiers against the *Be-don-ko-he* and the *Ned-ni.*"

"I am *Be-don-ko-he* — what you *pinda-likoye* call 'Cherry-cows.' "

McGivern nodded soberly. "They are brave fighters, greatly led."

The youth grunted. "You know our chiefs?"

"At San Carlos I drank *tulapai* with Cochise."

The youth's lips twisted faintly. "Cochise is a sick old man. His belly is sour with the white man's whisky."

"I led troops against Tana."

"What are you called?"

"McGivern."

67

"Ma-giv-urn. It is sour in my mouth. Your mouth is full of lies, I think." He stared bitterly at McGivern. "I am the grandson of Tana. Yours is not a name celebrated in our clan."

"Then try the name of Day-zen on your tongue, *ish-kay-nay;* it will taste truer."

The youth's eyes widened now; he raised his head, winced, and sank back against the saddle-blanket pallet. The Chiricahua warriors had long ago dubbed McGivern *dazen,* the Apache word for mule, because of his stubborn tenacity which had tracked down more than one war party. It was a name feared and respected, yet rarely spoken of with hatred, by the Apaches.

"How is the grandson of Tana called?"

"Gian-nah-tah."

They talked freely then, the Indian's bitter contempt evaporated before the white man all Apaches knew was not as other *pinda-likeoye* . . . an honored enemy in war, a fair-dealing friend in peace. After the last outbreak of hostilities, McGivern's recent reception at San Carlos had been cold, but this youth, whose garrulity with an enemy proved his free-wheeling ways, seemed unaware of the boycott. He spoke of old battles recounted by the elders, in which Mc-Givern had figured prominently; he mentioned warriors McGivern had met in peace and war.

McGivern did notice that Gian-nah-tah carefully veered from speaking of himself or his exploits, yet Apaches were notorious boasters. Nor did he make mention of Maco or his famous feud with the scout; and so McGivern was sure that Gian-nah-tah was one of the band dually led by Maco and Nachito. The Chiricahua was wary of betraying military secrets to a known enemy. McGivern wanted information, but he knew better than to press for it directly.

He was mulling over this as Gian-nah-tah asked suddenly: "Why did you spare my life? Has the heart of Day-zen turned to water?" He spat sideways. "Perhaps you have become a woman."

"I sprang, like Gian-nah-tah, from a woman's parts. Maybe it is that part, in me, that finds no warrior's honor in slaying the helpless."

Instead of the expected sneer, he saw a puzzled frown knit the Apache's forehead. "I understand — yet do not understand. When I see my brothers maiming and torturing small animals; when I see them drive white-hot king bolts into screaming white men as Maco —" Gian-nah-tah broke off at the slip of the tongue. "When I see these things," he went on slowly, "I feel a shame to which I cannot give a name, of my sire and his, and all my brothers. I do not mutilate, I do not torture. Once the others laughed, and their eyes said 'coward.' They do not laugh now," he finished grimly, as though he had said too much.

"Then we are alike," McGivern said quietly, and was silent, knowing men lost such a feeling by speaking too much of it. Gian-nah-tah said nothing, but his eyes held on McGivern's face with probing curiosity.

"I go now." McGivern pulled his cramped knees to a crouch. "I leave this." He indicated the canteen and a folded oilcloth containing a little jerked beef.

"And when you return?" Gian-nah-tah asked softly.

"When you are well, I take you to a white man's fort."

"I will be gone from here before another sun," Gian-nah-tah said matter-of-factly.

"You will not ride for a quarter of a moon. The wound will open and kill you."

A glint touched Gian-nah-tah's eyes, though he did not smile. "If we were at San Carlos, I would wager my best pony."

"Perhaps we will drink *tulapai* there."

"No." The calm matter-of-factness again. "If I return to San Carlos, it will be in death."

McGivern slung the saddlebags from his shoulder, crawled from the cave and stood erect on the outer ledge. He was surprised to see the far westering of the sun crowning the desert rim with rose-gold. The day's happenings had seemed crowded into a small time. He would not be seeing Belden's ranch by daylight now, he reflected coldly, and time might be running out. Tomorrow, then. Meanwhile he felt drained to exhaustion and ravenously hungry. There was food and a bed in Saguaro.

You're getting old, McGivern, he thought sourly, *or soft in more ways than one.*

70

7

It was full dark when McGivern reached Saguaro. After turning the sorrel in at the livery, he headed for the hotel to clean up. Two men were sitting on the front steps, their cigarettes glowing cherry-red. Their low talk broke off as he stepped onto the porch. Their heads turned to follow him, light from a lobby window crossing their faces. One was dark, narrow-shouldered, and sallow-faced; the other was chunky and straw-haired, with eyes like dirty ice. Both wore filthy denims and both returned McGivern's regard with tough, cynical stares.

McGivern tramped on past into the lobby, knowing they'd been waiting for him. *I'll be watched from here on,* he thought, and bleakly accepted that and let his mind run ahead of it. He went up to his room and washed, then slapped most of the dust from his clothes. Afterward, since it was past the hotel supper hour, he left for the Cattlemen's Cafe downstreet. He didn't have to glance back to know that the two men were following him.

The Cattlemen's was a spacious eatery with linen-covered tables, and looked clean enough. A few late patrons were still eating. McGivern took a corner table where he could watch the room. A harried-looking waitress took his order — a double helping of beef stew, apple pie, and a pot of coffee — then went to wait on the two toughs who'd taken a table near the door. The straw-haired one raised his wicked gaze. "Forget it, sister," he said flatly. The girl backed off, eyes wide, and hurried to the kitchen.

McGivern sat back to wait for his food, letting his gaze slowly travel the room. His eyes halted on a bald, enormously fat man in a loud waist-coat who appeared to be finishing off a whole roast chicken by himself. The fat man glanced over at the two toughs, then at McGivern — with open curiosity. His eyes were slate-colored, the coldest McGivern had ever seen.

When the girl brought his food, McGivern at-tacked it hungrily, ignoring the toughs and the fat man. He finished his pie leisurely, poured a third cup of coffee and lighted a cigar. The door opened and Reggie Harlan came in. He went di-rectly to the fat man's table and leaned toward him, talking in a low voice. The fat man cut him off with a word, nodding toward McGivern. Harlan turned in his chair, faint humor in his eyes as they met McGivern's. The fat one would be George Belden, McGivern now realized.

Harlan rose and came over to McGivern's table. "Pleasant ride, sport?" There was a pale malice in his eyes. "Like the country, do you?"

McGivern tapped cigar ash into a saucer. "It's not bad," he said idly. "I'd have to see more."

Reggie grinned derisively. "I'll bet."

72

"Those two clowns belong to you?"

Reggie's grin didn't alter. "If they do?"

"Pull them off," McGivern said softly. "I'm telling you."

"Free country, a man rides where he likes. Them as well as you."

"I wonder," McGivern murmured, "if they'd push over as easy as Pride."

"Pride jumped you, friend," Reggie said amiably. "You could have got the sheriff to serve a warrant and had Pride's heels cooling in the lock-up. Kruger and Mills ain't bothered you. Now you bother *them* —" He paused meaningfully. "Well, it's a nice, tight lock-up, friend."

"A nice tight frame-up."

"You said it, not me." Reggie chuckled. "See you in church, sport." He went back to Belden's table.

McGivern sat scowling at his empty plate, his cigar going cold between his fingers while his mind raced furiously over his dilemma. Reggie had plainly inferred that wherever he rode, the two gunnies would not be far away. If he chose them out, they'd have the sheriff pick him up. Even if he left the hotel by the back way and got his horse, the desk clerk and the livery hostler were both in Belden's pay. His tired mind picked at the problem confusedly. Maybe a drink would help; he stood, dropped a half-dollar on the table and walked out. Kruger and Mills were less than a dozen paces behind as he went through the batwings of the Belle Fourche. A girl was singing

73

in a clear soprano, and the men at the tables and bar were silent, their attention on her.

Pushing through the crowd, McGivern saw Georgette, nee Julia Lanphere, sitting on the far end of the bar, legs crossed and hand on her hip as she sang. McGivern ordered a drink, with Belden's toughs bellying up a yard away. The customers were respectfully silent and rapt as Georgette gave sweet, staid renditions of "Annie Laurie" and "Sweet Afton." Without changing the inflection or mood of her style, she launched into a bawdy trail-herders' ballad. She did not belt it out as you expected a casino singer to, and the men broke their silence with a roar of laughter.

A hand touched his arm. "Something, ain't she, Mac?"

"Evening, Ma. The clientele thinks so," McGivern said dryly.

Ma Gates' vast bosom stirred with her chuckle. "Honest to God, you ought to run for chairman of a civic busybody league. Your blood's gone deader'n flat beer."

"Age creeping up."

"My stars, don't I know it." Ma sighed. "But you . . . old?"

"Matter of fact," he smiled, "I was wondering if your singer would like more conversation with a beat-up old scout."

"Sounds more like McGivern," Ma grunted. "Sit yourself. I'll have her come to the table. All right?"

"Fine," he said absently. His mind was ticking

now; Georgette might be able to help him un-knowingly.

He ordered another drink and carried it to a table. Ma Gates moved over to speak to the girl; she nodded, giving McGivern a smile of recognition. She finished her song to wild applause and yells of "More, Georgie, more," and shook her head in cool refusal. A grinning cowboy swung her to the floor.

McGivern was on his feet holding a chair for her, and she slipped into it with a murmured, "Thank you." He took his seat opposite her, offered to buy a drink, which she declined, and cudgeled his brain for an amenity. He said uncomfortably that he'd liked her first songs.

"Thank you again."

"Even if you didn't like it much . . . up there."

Her candid eyes searched his face. "I've had cowhands pour out their troubles to me when they've drunk themselves past shyness. Then tell me I don't belong here . . . offer to take me away from all this. You are the first to notice how *I* felt, what I thought."

"That's true most anywhere." He shrugged. "Civilization hasn't got to the stage where men care what women feel — or they once did and have since stopped caring. Some of the tribes . . . the Cheyenne . . . admit women to council, value their advice."

Pleased surprise touched her face. "You think about these things. Now I am curious. Do you like to read?"

"Winter's the time when I read, when things slow down. No poetry or tea-time stuff, I'm afraid."

"But you have read seriously."

"When you spend a lot of time on the desert, alone, you think a lot. You want to learn more." He shifted with discomfort. This talk was as personal as he'd ever gotten with any woman . . . and he wasn't here for that. "Maybe you'd like to talk it over tomorrow morning. We could go riding. Though I haven't a buggy," he added, remembering Clyde Prentiss.

There was pleasure in her face, and a humorous understanding. "Why, I have riding clothes — and haven't had a chance to wear them."

"Tomorrow morning, then . . ." He let his voice trail, turning his head. Clyde Prentiss had just come in and was moving toward their table. He nodded to McGivern, a hint of displeasure on his sharp pale features.

"The usual ride tomorrow, Julia?" Prentiss asked curtly.

Her response was cool. "If I'm back in time. Mr. McGivern has asked me to ride with him; we're starting early."

"I see," Prentiss said primly, a flush mounting from his high collar. "Try not to be late, Julia." He turned without waiting for a reply, and stalked out.

She looked at McGivern, who said nothing. She colored slightly. "You're thinking that Clyde takes me for granted."

"Something like that."

She fingered a bracelet on her wrist, looking at it musingly. "Clyde and I come of the same background, though of different classes. Out here class doesn't matter." She looked up half-angrily, half-defensively. "If you can find three men in this town who've read five good books, have taste and at least occasional manners. . . ."

"I wasn't judging," McGivern said quietly. "Just thinking. My privilege. Yours too."

The stiffness relaxed from her face; she laughed, a little sharply. "At least you don't pretend you're not thinking."

He only nodded and stood up. "Tomorrow morning. I'll bring your horse here. About seven?"

"About nine," she said dryly. "I'm a late worker. At that, it will be early. Good night, Mr. McGivern."

Back in his hotel room, McGivern went to the window without lighting his lamp. Across the street, leaning against a gallery post of the Belle Fourche, was one of Belden's toughs, the light hitting his bare, tousled straw thatch. He was smoking, his head tilted back to watch Mc-Givern's window. They would watch the hotel in alternate shifts through the night, he guessed. Tomorrow both would be bleary and short-tempered from little sleep. Georgette — Julia — would help him do the rest.

8

"I believe those men are following us," Julia said calmly. She and Tom were a mile from Saguaro as she looked back across the flats, shading her eyes with her hand. She was wearing a green riding habit with a divided skirt. A matching porkpie hat was perched on her high-coiled pale hair, and she carried an Eastern riding crop.

"Pair of saloon loafers with nothing better to do," McGivern said idly.

"It does make you nervous, though. What an odd pastime. I never will understand Western man . . . In properly sloughing decorum," she added, "suppose you call me Julia."

"Tom, then, or Mac." To pull her attention from Kruger and Mills, he motioned with his hand. "Look there." Julia gave a little scream. A huge rattler was coiled in the shade of a shelving outcrop well to their right. "Let him alone," McGivern said, smiling, "and he'll let you alone."

"I — it startled me."

"This desert is a bigger book than you'll ever read, Julia. I've lived in it and I know it."

"I'd like to learn." Her eyes were bright as an eager child's, and somehow it was pleasing to see that her strangely mingled sophistication of

Beacon Hill and the Belle Fourche was only skin deep.

So he talked as they rode slowly through the gathering heat of midmorning, occasionally stopping to point out a giant *sahuaro* cactus, an unusual shrub or a darting lizard. Julia quickly and easily followed his shifting attention. It came to him with an unbidden suddenness that he was enjoying this, and he knew a twinge of guilt that he could be distracted for fleeting minutes from his mind-locked goal. Yet he knew that the timeless desert could work its own spell, erasing disillusion and hurtful memories as its healing herbs known by the Indians could alleviate physical sickness. They were two cynical people who needed that balm, but it was dangerous balm for a man and a woman alone. And McGivern thought: *Why not? The rest of it belongs to the past, the dead past. Maybe you're beginning to want to forget.*

His conscience flailed the thought, angrily denying it. He was all right now, he told himself; he straightened in his saddle, scanning the flat landscape. There was a jumbled rise of shale formations about two miles distant, he judged; imperceptibly he neck-reined his horse in that direction. Kruger and Mills were hanging back about a mile, easily keeping within eyeshot of these flats. The trick now was to lull their attention. . . .

It was close to noon when McGivern and Julia had ranged leisurely to the edge of the shale rise. The horses picked their way over the crumbling slate to a narrow height of land. Here McGivern halted, dismounted, and helped Julia down. He broke out sandwiches from his saddlebags, two cups, and a bottle of *rioja alta* wine.

"A little warm," he said in apology as they sat tailor-fashion on the warm rock and he poured the wine.

"But this is wonderful. I know wines, and this is a good one. How did you ever find it in Saguaro?"

"Got the hotel cook to put up the lunch. Learned he used to be a *chef de maître* in New Orleans. Came out here as a lunger. This is from his private stock. I thought it would please you."

"You're thoughtful, Tom. Thank you." She sipped the wine, her eyes fixing him disturbingly.

He looked away, across the shimmering flats. Kruger and Mills had dismounted from their horses and were squatting on the ground with smokes. They were bored and they were angry. They hadn't slept much, and they'd been riding a hot desert at a slow gait. Now they were hunkered down, with empty bellies, cursing Harlan and Belden and wondering why the hell they were trailing McGivern on a picnic outing with a honkytonk girl. They were undisciplined hellraisers, and this trailing took patience. McGivern guessed he could throw them off without difficulty; they'd look around half-heartedly, swear a little, then ride back to town and wait for him.

When he and Julia had finished eating, McGivern packed the saddlebags unhurriedly and told her "Let's lose those two."

She nodded, her eyes bright, and he thought uneasily that a heady combination of sun and wine was giving her the wrong idea, and she was not averse to it. They mounted and rode lengthwise across the height without haste and in plain view, McGivern in the lead. "Now," he said quietly, and abruptly put his horse down a steep incline. Shale rattled away ahead of him, and Julia gamely held his pace. He kicked his mount into a canter up a small canyon full of angled turns. The whole formation was crosshatched with miniature gorges, and McGivern led recklessly through the labyrinth, working toward the south and east.

Within a half hour they broke again onto open flats, and he called over his shoulder, "Let your horse out." They settled into a mile-eating gallop which McGivern shortly halted, knowing the horses could not weather such a pace in this heat.

Julia reined up beside him, laughing shakily. "That was fun."

"You haven't laughed before."

Her face sobered; she said gently, "I hadn't much to laugh about — before."

He hastily changed the subject. "Thought

we'd head south now, then swing back to town." Without waiting for her reply, he nudged the sorrel into motion. He meant to leave her at the town outskirts, then strike for Chain Anchor alone.

He could make out the great ridge formation that lay north of Belden's ranch, and he idly wondered how the wounded Apache was. He'd thought little of the Indian youth since yesterday. As a cog in Belden's intrigues, he was negligible; the Apaches could send another man, but at least the gun liaison was delayed. Aside from the seed of personal liking that had begun between them, he had no reason to concern himself further with Gian-nah-tah. He was still an enemy, and Mc-Givern had done no more than their common humanity dictated.

There was a more pressing concern to occupy his attention: locating the cache of Winchesters. That settled, he would return to the cave — and what? McGivern wondered cynically. Take the Apache to Belden's sheriff and Belden's jail in Belden's town? Or let him return to his war party to kill more whites? McGivern could not delay his self-imposed task of seeing the gun smuggling completely smashed, to take the Apache hundreds of miles to a fort. He shook his head wearily; moral decisions were infinitely more complicated than the black-and-white judgments made by his stiff-necked Covenanter parents.

The ridge rose nearer with their steady pace,

and now McGivern saw several buzzards wheeling against the brassy sky. For three minutes as they rode he watched the carrion birds swoop and hover and hesitate to settle; their prey was not yet dead. Without telling Julia, McGivern reined casually in that direction.

Shortly they topped a dune and looked into a small, brush-filled swale. Gian-nah-tah's paint stood there, placidly switching flies off its flanks. Yesterday McGivern had left the pony tethered in some shrubbery at the base of the ridge.

"What is it?" Julia asked sharply.

McGivern didn't answer. He slid from his saddle and ran down the slope. Gian-nah-tah was sprawled on his face in the brush at the bottom of this swale to which his desertcraft had guided him before his strength failed. His clawed fingers sunk in scrabbled clay showed where he'd started to dig for water. Exertion had reopened his wounds; fresh bloodstains welted the flannel bandage. McGivern ran back to his horse and fetched his canteen. He turned Gian-nah-tah's limp body on its back, supporting the boy's head against his arm as he tilted the canteen to his lips. The Apache stirred; his eyes opened and his throat muscles worked convulsively. McGivern let him have a few swallows, then corked his canteen and set it aside.

As his head was turned, Gian-nah-tah exploded beneath him. McGivern was flung joltingly on his side and like a striking snake the

Chiricahua was on him, snatching McGivern's knife from its hip sheath. The blade made a silvery arc in the sun as his arm went back. For a moment it hung in the air like Julia's startled scream, and in that moment McGivern grabbed the wiry wrist and twisted.

Gian-nah-tah groaned, weakly trying to smother McGivern's leverage with his leaning weight, and the Apache smell that was grease and sweat and woodsmoke was rank and full in McGivern's face. An upsweep of his arm would have smashed his elbow cruelly into Gian-nah-tah's wounded side. Instead McGivern scissored his legs around the Apache's hips and rolled him aside. With another hard twist he forced Gian-nah-tah to release the knife. He snatched it up and sprang to his feet. Gian-nah-tah lay on his back panting, eyes filled with pain.

"It was a good try, *pinda-likoye*," he whispered. "I will not go back to San Carlos — alive."

McGivern sheathed his knife. "A fool try, *ish-kay-nay*. You might have reached San Carlos alive — with me — had you waited in the cave. You would not have made it back to Maco's band alone. You almost died here."

"In the night a fever ate my brain; I drank all the water you left, and still my thirst raged. You did not return; shall a warrior die in a hole like a wounded animal?"

Gian-nah-tah struggled slowly to his feet, disdaining McGivern's extended hand. He backed

84

off at an unsteady pace, almost falling. Then with a burst of reserve energy that again caught McGivern off-guard, Gian-nah-tah wheeled, swift as thought, sprang to the paint and snatched the Winchester from its buckskin sheath. He wheeled back in the same movement, leveling the rifle, but McGivern had already palmed up and cocked his pistol. Yesterday McGivern had cached the Apache's weapons under a flat rock near the pony; evidently Gian-nah-tah had easily found them.

The Apache grinned wolfishly. "What do you call this, Day-zen?"

"The white-eyes call it a Mexican stand-off."

"No. If you were a *nak-kai-ye,* we would both shoot." He meant the hereditary hatred between the Mexicans and the Apaches. "There is liking between us."

McGivern nodded watchfully. "Yet you tried to kill me, as I would in your place . . . The liking counts for nothing here."

"A little, maybe. Also we are neither of us fools. I shall withdraw now, and neither will shoot, for both will surely die. Another day we may fight and one shall die. Or, if Yusn wills, in a better time I will take the hand I refused."

McGivern shook his head. "To come this far, you almost died. Another mile will finish you."

Gian-nah-tah's right hand braced the ready rifle against his hip as he inched forward to McGivern's canteen on the ground between them. With a swift movement he lifted it, slung the strap to his shoulder and straightened. "Your water gave back my life; it will keep me alive till I reach my people."

He backed to his horse and swung astride, bowing with a wince of pain across his horse's mane. "It is a great thing to fox Day-zen twice. *Adios.*" The Apache sidled his horse away a good thirty paces, bent low over the withers, and quirted the paint into a run toward the north. He had brains to match his courage, and he was an Apache; he would win through. McGivern didn't want to think about that. He'd unwarily let free an enemy who could kill more whites.

He tramped up the slope to where Julia waited wide-eyed, her reins twisted between her hands. As he stepped into his saddle, she burst out, "What happened between you and him?"

McGivern shrugged. "You saw the story. A standoff."

She shook her head slowly, her eyes puzzled. "You knew each other before. Why — he was almost friendly!"

"Knew him at San Carlos. I lived there once."

"I believe that . . . the way you knew the language . . . but I think there's more. I think those two men were following us for a reason. I think that wounded Apache was here for a reason. I think, Mr. McGivern, that you even brought me with you for a reason."

Her words were firm with conviction, edged with a faint scorn. McGivern's face felt hot at her accuracy. "Anything else?"

"Yes. I think you're too friendly with a hostile. I've seen peaceful Apaches. Didn't he wear the paint designs of a hostile?"

McGivern nodded wearily; she would have to know it all now, knowing as much as she did and putting a wrong interpretation on it. Yet how far could he trust a woman he'd met two days ago?

He talked as they headed their horses back toward Saguaro, telling in a toneless, factual way everything that had happened since he'd received a telegram from Colonel Cahill over three months ago. She rode without looking at him, but watching her face now and again he saw the tenseness relax and shades of concerned emotion replace it.

When he'd finished they jogged on in a full minute's silence, before Julia spoke in a hushed voice. "This girl . . . you knew her for a long time, Tom?"

"Since we were kids," he said quietly. "Our families had neighboring farms in Ohio. When I reached eighteen, my feet got too itchy; I had to ride out and see the world. Ann understood — and she said she'd wait. I hit the deep West, and what with one thing and another I forgot that I'd ever promised to come back. Thirteen years. Then, a year ago, my freight business was prospering and I got an urge to go back to Ohio. Mostly, that was a mistake. Mam and Pap were dead, my old friends were strangers."

He paused humbly. "But Ann had waited. At least, she hadn't forgotten, as I had."

"I don't quite understand," Julia said in soft admission. "It isn't human nature to just . . . wait."

McGivern looked at her quickly, his glance a little hard. "That's your judgment, an easy one. You're a beautiful woman. She wasn't pretty, even as a girl. She was thirty-one when I went back."

"A lot of women marry who aren't attractive," Julia said defensively. But she added thoughtfully, "I suppose a plain girl would find it easier . . . to wait."

"Waiting is never easy," he said flatly. "I know this: I went back. And she was there. And it was the same between us again. She had a beauty that . . ." He stopped, searching for words. "It wasn't so easy to see because it was inside."

"The only kind that counts," Julia murmured. There was reluctance that was almost pain in her words that made him look at her strangely.

There was another silence before she spoke again, the brittleness sharply accenting her voice. "I was a vain, fuzzy-minded little girl once, my friend; all that, though I was nineteen. Beacon Hill upper crust, and a minister's daughter at that. Our life was luxurious, yet conservative, and always you lived by the book. Not the Scriptures, the social register. There were rules and rules. I tired of them all."

She hesitated, her tongue touching her lips. "There was a musician, a traveling European pianist, who played concerts in drawing rooms. I met him at a party. He was continental to the core, with dark sad eyes and long pale hands. He coughed a great deal — what you call 'a lunger,' I suppose — and he spouted long stanzas of unintelligible verses in French: he called himself an aesthetic rebel. Being what I told you, I used to meet him secretly in a rose-petal-and-pink-tea haze. And when he left Boston, I went with him."

She smiled palely. "We were married in the first town we came to, if that's important. I soon found Raoul drank when the coughing fits became too severe. And when he drank, he . . . never mind. One night in Albany after a concert, he shot himself through the head." She turned her head away, looking across the desert. "They said the West was a new land for a new start. I found one here . . . of sorts."

"Your family," McGivern said quietly.

"I wrote letters. They all came back with a concise note. To the effect that the Reverend Mr. Jonathan Lanphere no longer had a daughter. She ran off with an immoral 'show person,' and so ceased to exist." She shook her head in puzzled bitterness. "Well, the life isn't so bad by some standards. I have my honor, whatever that means, and I eat three meals a day. I don't ask for pity; for five years I've weltered in self-pity till I'm sick of it. And of myself."

McGivern was silent now as the buildings of Saguaro came into view. *Not bad by some standards.* Yet by contrast with a Beacon Hill upbringing, he could see casino life would tear a sensitive, well-bred woman apart. As it would Julia unless, somehow, she freed herself.

He reined in behind a swell of low dunes, and she looked at him questioningly. "I'm riding to Belden's ranch," he said. "What happens there is my business. I'll have to trust you, Julia."

"I'll keep your secret." She smiled tiredly. "You keep mine — no, more; forget it. I'm sorry. I had to tell someone, that was all."

"You can bottle a thing up just so long," he agreed softly. "But I won't forget, Julia."

"Strange. I know that you rode with me today under a pretense, and yet I find myself telling you everything." She watched him a concerned moment. "You'll be careful, Tom . . ." She reined her horse quickly away, heading for town.

McGivern watched her until she was out of sight beyond the dunes, then swung east again at a brisk clip. In an hour he achieved the hogback and the southward-running canyon which bisected it. He rode warily into the winding gorge, ready for anything; Chain Anchor might have outriders patrolling the drift lines, and if they'd been expecting an Apache contact, they'd know by now that something had gone wrong. Wariness heightened when he found fresh sign where a lone shod horse had traversed the canyon only hours ago, then turned back. Perhaps Harlan himself, though it wasn't likely he'd unriddled what had happened.

The canyon ended high on the far side of the ridge and spilled down in a broken shale slide to its base. The character of the land altered sharply, as though the ridge made a clean demarcation between the desert to its north and the grassy plains here that undulated away to south and east. The ridge was Chain Anchor's northern range boundary, McGivern guessed as he halted at the canyon exit; a several-branched creek sparkled between the richly grassed hills, the source of their fertility.

He had to spur the sorrel to braving the treacherous slide, and at its bottom he immediately struck due south through the grass, following the faint ruts of the wagon trail. For an hour he rode steadily, spooking up occasional bunches of decrepit or half-wild steers ranging along the creek bottoms. All bore the brand of an anchor with two chain links. Obviously Belden hadn't driven to market for several years, and his neglected ranch was, as Ma Gates had said, only a cover-up.

Ahead, the land rose to a low wooded ridge where McGivern dismounted and tethered his horse. He cat-footed through the trees to the summit of the slope. He could see into the gradual dip of a wide bowl where Chain Anchor headquarters lay.

The low ridge formed a timber-cloaked horseshoe, enclosing the ranch on three sides, but open to the west. His vantage was from the north arm of the horseshoe. The bowl flattened off at the bottom in a vista of rolling park dotted with big isolated cottonwoods. The thick, rich lawn that surrounded the buildings might once have been well-tended, but now the grass was knee-deep and rank, and the near buildings, a bunkhouse, a cookshack, and a maze of barns, sheds, the pole corrals, showed a careless lack of repair.

The main house was built of massive timbers, flanked by wings of fieldstone. It, along with a carriage shed and stables, was set off at the entrance to the horseshoe. Unlike the working part of the ranch, with its look of weatherbeaten neglect, the owner's part was well-kept, with trimmed hedges, a gravel drive, and a well-clipped lawn.

McGivern took stock of it all, charting it indelibly in his mind as he hunkered down in the timber above to wait out the day. He saw little activity. Some crewmen were loafing on a bench in front of the bunkhouse, apparently with nothing to do. A red-haired woman in a print dress came out of the big house and sat in the porch swing. McGivern had seen her in town yesterday morning, talking to the sheriff; curiously, he wondered what her place here was. From this distance she looked slender and youthful, surely not the wife of the gross, aging Belden. His daughter or housekeeper, probably.

Toward sunset a buggy accompanied by two horsemen drove in from the west along the town road and turned in at the gravel drive. Mc-

Givern identified Belden in the buggy, flanked by Harlan and Sheriff Paul Hornbeck. The girl rose and met them on the steps, and all went inside.

The vultures are gathering, was McGivern's wry thought, and he guessed that the missing Apache contact, and his own possible role in the Apache's failure to show up, would be the center of the discussion. His nerves were beginning to hairtrigger, and he called on his old stolid patience to wait till darkness. Tonight, if a gun cache was on this ranch, he would find it. And when he was through with the rifles, none would be usable by the Apaches or anyone else.

9

Julia returned her horse to the livery stable and walked slowly back to the Belle Fourche. She felt slack and bone-weary, and knew that tomorrow she would pay with a hundred aches and twinges for these unaccustomed hours in the saddle. But now the weariness was a pleasant one, permeating body and mind with a deep restfulness. Men turned to stare as she went by, and she thought, *I must be a sight.* Her green habit was covered with dust; her skin felt sweaty and gritty, pleasantly so. A lifetime as a society and saloon prima donna had cut her off from such direct sensations.

It wasn't till she turned in at the side door of the Belle Fourche and started up the stairway to her room that she learned why the men had stared. Ma Gates met her at the head of the stairwell, hands at hips, regarding her with amazement.

"God's sake, Georgie. Expected you to be wore out, and here you're pert as fresh daisies. Just a little sunburned. You look great. What'n hell happened?"

"Why — nothing," Julia said in confusion. "Your friend is quite a gentleman."

Ma grunted. "You can't tell me nothin' about

Tom McGivern. The mouse was here an hour ago, askin' after you."

"Clyde?" She'd forgotten about Clyde. "What did he want?"

"Asked if you was back from your ride with that McGivern person." Ma grunted furiously. "Damned hoity-toity runt. Sent him packin' with red ears."

Julia felt a swift irritation that Clyde had been probing at her personal life in his sly way. Then she remembered she'd promised him the usual buggy ride when he finished work. "I have an engagement, Mrs. Gates. Could you have Charley bring hot water up?"

"Best rest, girl," Ma snapped. "You got to go to work at six. Can't have my girls' personal lives pushing on their work."

"I'm sorry, Mrs. Gates. I promised."

Ma grumbled as Julia went on to her room, but Julia heard her bawl for Charley the swamper to ready up a hot bath for Georgette. Behind a screen, she struggled with the buttons of her limp riding habit, while Charley, a hunchbacked old derelict, brought up buckets from the kitchen and filled a washtub improvised for the girls' baths. Afterward she locked her door, slipped into the tub and let the water slide like a hot soothing cloak over her. She closed her eyes, enjoying the sense of languid ease. Not the least of it was due to unburdening herself to McGivern; she hadn't realized how badly she'd needed to tell someone all. It had seemed oddly natural to unburden herself to this man she hardly knew.

She had never considered telling Clyde Prentiss of her past; Clyde had already guessed much of it, and she was too used to his iron judgments in moral matters. She could always retaliate by deliberately saying things to shock him, though at times she thought there was a sly, ferocious hypocrisy behind Clyde's prim front.

Distastefully she put Clyde out of mind, and smiled secretly, enjoying the tingling warmth that was not wholly from the hot water. She'd thought she would never have any more illusions about men, yet she had known the old romantic stirrings of girlhood today. The desert, the wine, the incident with the Apache, had all contributed — but she couldn't deny that all these had centered about the man at her side, releasing a torrent of long pent-up feeling in her. *You're a fool,* she thought suddenly, bitingly; *you were nothing but a pretty accessory to him, and now you know why he is here and what he is fighting. A man alone against all Belden's crooked power. You will probably not see him again . . . not alive.*

A fear almost like a physical sickness struck her. She stepped from the tub, toweled briskly, automatically selected a dress from her closet. She thought with distaste of the hour ahead with Clyde Prentiss. Usually she nostalgically enjoyed his knowledgeable range of talk, from business to Emerson's philosophy and the novels of Hawthorne, all related in his crisp Massachusetts nasality; but today she viewed the prospect of the next hour with him as almost unbearable. Should she plead a headache? But McGivern had put his trust in her; she must behave naturally and graciously, particularly to Clyde, whose ferreting curiosity and jealousy already filled him with unspoken suspicion of McGivern. Then, she thought, Clyde worked for George Belden; how deeply was he immersed in the man's enterprises?

She was ready at the side door when Clyde reined his buggy in front at exactly three o'clock, stepped down and came briskly up the alley. He halted on the steps, eyes widening with almost reluctant admiration. "I must say, Julia, that you've never looked lovelier."

"Thank you, Clyde," she murmured in quiet concealment of her lack of pleasure. Yet he seemed to sense this and was silent as he handed her to the seat, took up the reins, and crisply put the livery bays into motion. Clyde took a western road from town, which followed a sluggish, cottonwood-bordered creek. He halted in the dappled shade, jabbed the buggy whip back in its socket with a sharp motion and turned a disapproving face to her.

"I hadn't mentioned it before, Julia; it was none of my business. But do you think it best that you see this McGivern so regularly? The man is rough, semiliterate, at best. Not," he added hastily, "that this is an index to his true character. But he *is* a stranger of whom we know nothing —"

"As you say, Clyde, it's none of your business," she said tartly. "However, Mrs. Gates knows him — most approvingly."

"That old harridan —" Clyde began, but a stormy hint in Julia's glance cut him off. He looked sullenly down the creek, nervously fingering the reins. Julia was satisfied to let him stew. A good share of their relationship was built on tacit or spoken conflict which amused her. But now she was not amused, only bored and angry. . . .

Back in Boston, Clyde would have been of the serving class that clerked in the stores patronized by her wealthy relatives; in this blunt land where even the cattle baron was often on first-name terms with his sorriest puncher, she knew that much of Clyde's attraction to her was a sense of class which would have been off-limits to him back East. His occasional hints of marriage, which she deftly fended off, were founded, she guessed, on a vicarious thrill the staid bookkeeper received from consorting with a debutante-turned-casino-singer, and the sense of righteousness he would receive from lifting her to respectability — on his terms. It would satisfyingly wipe out the ingrained inferiority he couldn't help feeling, and out of sheer gratitude she would become a demure and decorous wife.

So much for Clyde, she thought a trifle

grimly; her own feelings she had already summed up. That left McGivern, the cause of their immediate bickering. McGivern, who'd left her and headed into danger, perhaps death; and she could do nothing for him. The clammy fear came back like an icy blow in the stomach. If only there were a safe way for him to collect the evidence he needed to smash the gunrunners. . . .

Maybe there is. The thought was like another blow, bright and relieving. Clyde Prentiss might be humanly small, but she had no reason to doubt his honesty; wasn't he forever prating of business ethics and some employers' lack of them? There was something mealy-mouthed in the way he hinted at George Belden's underhandedness, which he would never dare mention to Belden's face. But no man who'd never achieved the depths of depravity could condone gunrunning; Clyde's ignorance was almost certain, yet he was in a position to undermine the vicious operation.

She turned suddenly to him. "Clyde, have you received any large shipments of Winchester rifles lately? Were they noted in the company books?"

He swung his head, facing her warily. "What brought on that question?"

Julia hesitated only a moment before telling him, slowly and carefully, that George Belden was almost certainly running guns to an Apache band. For proof, she drew on all McGivern had told her about his experiences since arriving in Saguaro, omitting his true reason for coming here, explaining that he was acting at the Army's behest, and had traced large shipments of Winchesters to Saguaro.

"I see," Clyde murmured when she had finished. All animosity had vanished, and his voice was sharp with interest. "Strange. We've received a number of sizable crates of the sort used to pack rifles at intervals during the last months. I've watched the yard men unload them. Once a crate broke open and spilled out its load — yes, new Winchesters." He stroked his chin thoughtfully, repeating, "Strange. The crates were always transferred to a yard warehouse, yet I've often been in that warehouse and found no rifles in storage. I assumed they must have been taken away after I was off work, almost with an air of secrecy. They were not distributed to local merchants — and the Army doesn't contract for Winchesters. There was never mention of them on invoices, no record entered in my book. Of course all this seemed odd, but it isn't discreet to question an employer too closely. And I know nothing of gunrunners or their methods; it never occurred —" He broke off flatly, his eyes narrowed and cautious. "Of course, you had a reason for asking."

"Yes, Clyde," she said steadily. "I want you to write the commandant at Fort Laughlin — Colonel Cahill, Tom McGivern's friend. I want you to tell him what you told me. It should be enough to warrant a full investigation of George Belden's freighting activities and his company's books . . . perhaps enough to bring him to trial . . . with your testimony of what you know. Some of the teamsters must be honest men who can corroborate that the guns *were* delivered. Neither Tom nor the Army can do anything on mere suspicion — but your testimony as Belden's bookkeeper —"

"Would save risk to Mr. McGivern's precious neck, eh, Julia?"

"Don't be small, Clyde!" she said vehemently. "Don't think small, for heaven's sake — where the lives of hundreds of innocent people are at stake. You haven't been out here long; you haven't lived close to an Indian uprising. I have. It's horrible!"

"Yes," Prentiss said softly, musingly, as though her vehemence hadn't touched him. "All right, Julia. I'll see what I can do. I'll check the books over again, tonight, to make certain. I have an office passkey for night work."

"See me afterward. Tell me what you found out."

He nodded, clucked to the horses and swung their buggy around, headed back for town. Julia afforded herself only a slight relief. McGivern was still in danger, until she could tell him of Clyde's agreement to help. *Let him come back,* she prayed. *Let him come soon.*

10

Crouched in the brush on the ridge, McGivern slowly chewed a strip of jerky, let the tough, fibrous mouthful slide down his throat. He smiled wryly at this old ritual. Town life softened a man, yet he'd often lived for weeks on jerky and a little water. Down below, lights shone in the main house. Belden and his group would be finishing supper, and the crew had finished straggling back from the bunkhouse.

It was full dark and time to move. He left concealment and worked down the slope, coming up behind the wall of the nearest shed. He hugged the wall, edging to its far corner. A thorough search of rambling sheds might consume hours, but he had the whole night.

He started to ease around the corner, then flattened to the wall as the door of the huge hay barn creaked open a scant twenty yards away. A man stepped out, paused to shape a cigarette and light it. Then he paced on, headed for the bunkhouse, a rifle swinging from his hand. *That's it,* McGivern thought with a stir of excitement. *The barn. That was a guard.* He was lucky, but he could have been as unlucky, if he'd entered the barn and run full into the guard. This must be a change of shifts, and the relief would be along shortly. He'd have to work fast.

McGivern melted through the shadows to the double doors which the guard had neglected to close. Just inside, he struck a match and hand-cupped its flare away from the doorway. The wash of light before the flare died to a steady flame showed him a bare clay floor, a loft above with a wooden ladder. He pinched out the match and in utter darkness took two steps that brought him to the ladder. He groped for a rung and started to climb. When he felt the board floor of the loft, he swung his weight up and forward and crouched at its edge, listening.

Satisfied, he struck another match. In its feeble flicker he saw a pile of hay against a far wall. He stood, bending his tall frame under the low rafters, and moved to the hay. He swept his foot through it, encountering the hollow side of a box. He stooped and pulled away the hay, exposing four long rectangular cases. There were no stamps or identifying marks, he saw before the match singed his fingers and went out. Carefully he struck another, pulled his knife from its sheath, drove the blade under the slatted cover of the topmost box, and pried upward. There was a thin shriek of nails, and he stopped, holding his breath, listening to the silence. Then, getting purchase with his fingertips, he lifted the cover.

They were there . . . spanking new Winchester '73's tiered in compact rows. This was what he had come to find. There was no time to wreck each one systematically by dislodging the firing pin, as he'd planned; he had to think of getting out before the guard was renewed. He extinguished the match, moved back to the loft edge, and there froze to immobility.

A man's booted steps were moving casually across the trampled ranchyard toward the barn. He couldn't get out in time; he'd wait for the guard to take up his position and then get the drop on him. He slipped his .45 from its holster, with the bleak knowledge that the guard could identify him to Belden, and from then on McGivern would be free game in an open field for Belden's gunnies. If he escaped the ranch. . . .

Unsteady lantern glow filled the doorway as the guard approached, and then he stepped inside, a tall, wavering shadow in the saffron glow. He paused in the doorway to glance around, the high-held lantern illumining his battered face. It was Pride Bloom, hat cuffed back on his greasy hair. A dirty bandage laid a grimy streak across his broken nose. McGivern watched tensely from the loft shadow as Pride walked to the ladder, shifting his rifle to the hand that held the lantern, holding both awkwardly as he reached up to grab the ladder rung with his free hand.

McGivern leaned out to view, pistol leveled. "Hold it there. Keep that hand up and stand off."

Pride jerked, looked up, and then took two steps back, his arms stiffly erect. "Do it all slow. Pull your sidearm and drop it," McGivern ordered. Pride did so, unspeaking as his malignant gaze picked out and identified McGivern. "The rifle. Reach out and get it with your free hand, drop it. Now lower that lantern to the floor and straighten up with your hands high."

Pride obeyed, still wordlessly. McGivern, still facing Pride, started to swing down to the top rung to descend. In that instant, with McGivern's body twisted awkwardly, Pride's foot lashed out, hit the lantern and sailed it against a supporting post. The light shattered and died. McGivern held his fire and then, hearing Pride scramble for his guns, leaped off into the darkness, hitting the clay floor lightly, pivoting to face Pride's gunflash. The shot made an echoing boom, the slug hammering into the wall at McGivern's back. At the end of his pivot, pulling his gun with him in a tight arc, McGivern saw Pride outlined against the lesser darkness of the doorway. Then he fired.

Pride jerked back with the slug's impact, but somehow kept his feet. He shot again, blindly, and fired a third time as his legs gave and he went down on his face, gunflame blistering the floor ahead of his falling body. McGivern ran for the door, slipping to one knee on the wet clay and hearing a shout from the bunkhouse before he regained his feet and whipped out the door. Careening on his heel, he charged across the open yard for the slope. Lantern light spilled out the bunkhouse door as a flood of men poured through.

Shots buffeted the night. The close whir of a lead hornet told McGivern he was seen, and he dived sideways, into the deep and pooling shadows of a shed. On his hands and knees he skirted the wall, hugging its shadow, and came against a pole fence which ended at the shed corner. He heard confused shouts, as he slipped between the fence poles. He glanced back and saw additional lanterns and lamps bobbing across the yard now as the men fanned out. Reggie Harlan's voice was raised in a question, then roared orders.

McGivern backed off from the fence, came against something yielding and warm that snorted with fear and sprang away. *It's the horse corral*, he thought. Now the nearing lamplight picked out the shadowy forms of the horses, milling nervously, and he moved swiftly and noiselessly among them, crouching low as he worked across the corral. In the uncertain light, crouching groundward amid the milling horses, he misjudged his direction. Suddenly he came up against the fence, and instead of attaining the slope side and the safe darkness beyond, he saw more sheds beyond the fence.

Cursing under his breath, he started to step through the poles, and then two men jogged his way, circling the corral on this side with a lantern picking out their path. He drew his leg back, shot a glance around and saw the black hulk of a water trough. He dived, hit the dirt behind it and lay motionless as the two men ran past, a bare yard away, their lantern making a brief tawny aura around the narrow pocket of shadow that hid him, and then receding. He came to his feet and slipped out between the poles, making for a shed a few feet away.

He ducked through the low doorway and sank into a corner, his heart pounding. The darkness was heavy with the smell of coiled leather, and he knew that this was the harness shed. He couldn't stay here; soon Harlan would be organizing a search of each building.

Cautiously he edged to the doorway, gun palmed and ready. The bobbing flare of lanterns told him that the search was temporarily concentrating toward the shed where they'd last seen him, and now was the time to move. He looked out — and stepped quickly back at sight of a vague figure approaching the shed from the main house, walking fast. He flattened against the wall by the door; he could only wait for the man to enter, buffalo him fast, and then make a run for it.

The figure paused in the doorway. McGivern's hand shot out and caught a handful of collar, his fist tensed to strike. There was a muffled little scream. He released the woman at once, shoved her aside, swung and broke for the door.

She caught his arm and he started to shake her off, but instantly froze when he heard her sharp, imperative whisper: "Be still! Be quiet! They saw me; they're coming."

"Who's in there?" Harlan bellowed.

The woman brushed past McGivern, stepping out into the nearing lantern glow. "It's me," she said calmly.

McGivern heard Harlan halt, heard the hesitation as he digested this, the disgusted anger in his reply. "You picked a hell of a time to go riding."

"That would be entirely my business and none of yours. What is all this?"

"A prowler . . . around somewhere. Better get back to the house till we find him."

"I'll ask for your advice when I want it, and that will be never," she said tartly.

"Have it your way," Reggie said surlily, and McGivern heard him move off, bellowing more orders.

The woman stepped back to the doorway. "Make your run now," she whispered urgently. McGivern moved past her and circled the shed, fading like a shadow into the brush that backed it. A scraggly overgrowth of trees and thickets covered his retreat to the slope and its dense timber. He was safe now; the sounds and lanterns of the searchers were thinning away as he climbed the dark slope and found his unerring way down its opposite side to his tethered horse. Here he waited till he was certain the search for him was being confined to headquarters proper. Then he mounted, started to rein north.

An instinctive thought caused him to feel for the knife in his hip sheath, and the cold realization that it was not there made him rein in. In his haste to uncover the guns, he'd left the knife in the loft. It would surely be found, but only possibly would it be identified as his. He bleakly considered this and then shrugged. His knife would make little difference to Belden and Harlan in fixing the prowler's identity; they would suspect nobody but him. He thought briefly of Pride Bloom, knowing his bullet had been a fatal hit, and felt only a slight regret. Pride had been a human wolf, like his friend Jack Hurdy.

Starting to squeeze the sorrel into motion, he checked himself at the soft whicker of a horse nearby. He listened intently and picked out only the usual nocturnal sounds. Yet a horse was close by and he placed it in an island of timber below the tip of the ridge's north arm. Perhaps a stray animal . . . yet he was prompted to dismount and leg it toward the grove.

He wormed easily, noiselessly, between cottonwood boles free of underbrush. At the heart of the grove lay a small clearing, and in the hazy light of the moon now topping the eastern horizon he saw a standing horse, its reins trailing, in the center of the clearing. A man sat on a rock, nervously puffing a cigarette, face shadowed by his hatbrim. Even as McGivern sank to his haunches, eyes narrowed in puzzlement, he heard a horse plowing through the grove opposite to where he crouched.

The man heard it too; he stood swiftly, grinding his cigarette under his heel, and the moonlight caught on his gaunt face. Sheriff Paul Hornbeck. He must have come straight here from Belden's house, McGivern reasoned, but who was he waiting for? The approaching rider broke from the trees and swung down at the clearing's edge. It was the woman who had helped him; she wore a dark riding habit and her shining auburn hair was bared to the moonlight. She came forward to meet Hornbeck, running the last few steps into his arms.

There was a moment's silence, then her voice, released on a ragged breath: "I can't stand it any more, Paul . . . his indifference, his smug inferences —"

"He — he knows about us?" Hornbeck said thinly.

"Harlan saw us together, and Harlan is his eyes and ears. He knows that much, suspects the rest. And he doesn't even care. But he torments me with his oily hints. He sickens me. Everything about him is disgusting. Paul, if you care at all, you won't leave me under his roof another night!"

Hornbeck swallowed audibly. He took her arms, moved her gently away. "What do you want me to do, Melissa?"

"Not fight him, Paul. Just come away with me. All we need are two horses and some food and water."

"But what would we do, where would we go?"

"Anywhere, away from him!" Her words were a bitter, vehement outpour. "Paul, for once in

110

your life, stand up and fight for something you want! Don't hide behind that mock star you wear, don't crawl behind a bottle —"

She broke off at something she saw in his face, then added softly: "Paul, Paul, I'm sorry. But you don't know; you haven't been married to George Belden for fifteen years."

"Lissa, you're the only thing I ever cared for," Hornbeck said in a dogged, tormented way. "You must know that's why I really quit drinking." It was a rare moment of honesty for the man, McGivern guessed.

"I gave you that much," she said tonelessly. "But no more?" He was silent and she made a small, weary gesture. "Well, I don't blame you. Anyway — he'd find us, no matter how far we went."

"It wouldn't be right, Lissa." Hornbeck's voice was low, shamed.

"You need to believe that, don't you?" she said gently. "Neither of us can help what we are . . . and talking only makes it worse. You'd better go."

He gave her a brief, almost hungry, look and walked with slumped shoulders to his horse; stepped into the saddle. "When will I see you again?"

"Does it matter? Good night, Paul."

She stood in mid-clearing, head bowed, unmoving as Hornbeck wheeled his horse into the dense hedge of trees. When the sounds of his going had died away, McGivern rose and stepped into the clearing.

"I forgot to thank you, Mrs. Belden."

She turned, a startled hand lifting to her mouth. Surprise altered to a bitter, defiant stare as he crossed the clearing to her. "You have a strange way of thanks — Mr. McGivern, isn't it? — eavesdropping and having the gall to let me know it."

"I'm here by chance. Since it happened, I'll ask why you helped me."

She gave a slight, indifferent shrug. "I only know you're George's enemy. Anything that hurts my husband is worth helping."

"Yes'm. How much do you know about his activities?"

A braided riding quirt dangled from her wrist. Irritably she slapped it against her skirt. "That they're mostly crooked, and only gossip tells me that much. George is careful to see that I learn nothing that could be used against him. He keeps his private papers and all legal documents locked in his company safe. Don't waste time pumping me; I'd help you if I could — but I can't."

"Maybe," he murmured. "What can you tell me about Hornbeck?"

"Paul?" Her tone was guarded and defensive. "What do you want to know about Paul?"

"How deep he is with your husband," McGivern said bluntly.

"Oh." She laughed shortly, almost deprecatingly. "Paul is a tool, only. He hears the same gossip I do, and pretends he hears nothing. George, you see, gave him respectability — and Paul feels guilty because of me. He can't believe, still, that George is as black as I paint him. Paul is quite honest. Just — weak."

"And you, Mrs. Belden?"

"What of me, Mr. McGivern?"

"You live on with a man you despise."

A wry, painful smile touched her lips. "Oh, yes — *my* weakness. It's simple enough. I've stayed with George because one doesn't easily outgrow a silken and perfumed girlhood . . . and I lack for nothing, in that way. But you can give up anything — if you become desperate enough."

McGivern regarded her with mounting curiosity. In spite of the faint lines around her eyes and mouth, she was still a beautiful woman; the soft accents of the old South tempered her tones with a hint of antebellum graciousness. "I'm puzzled, ma'am. That's why you married him?"

"You're overcurious, sir," she said stiffly.

"About people, always."

Surprisingly, she gave a small, relaxed laugh. "That's honest, anyway. You're a strange man, Mr. McGivern, in that you invite confidence . . . Would you like to hear the silly story of a silly girl? My family's holdings were ransacked and burned by Sherman's army. George was just one of many carpetbagger politicians who came in to prey on the leavings. Even if my Southern pride hadn't been humbled by poverty — well — fifteen years ago, George was

113

quite handsome in a mature, fortyish way. And I was only eighteen, starry-eyed and ripe for the plucking. Too late, I realized he was completely cold and grasping, that he married me for my social value alone. So I languish in luxury on an isolated ranch, waiting to be used again when circumstance is ripe. George can't afford to lose me; no other woman would have him now, for love *or* money."

"Least of all one as beautiful, ma'am."

"Why — thank you." She flushed faintly. "I'm still a starry-eyed fool, you see; I like to hear nonsense from a man."

"The simple truth." He touched his hat. "Thanks. You've been a help."

"I have? How?"

"Hornbeck. He's not so tangled with Belden he can't free himself. And he's the law. I may need his help."

She shook her head with a small, sad smile. "Paul is hopeless. I wish it were otherwise. I haven't only been seeing him because I wanted him to take me away. I'm foolish enough to think that together we could have salvaged what's left of our lives. But Paul —"

McGivern interrupted. "There aren't many drunks who can quit, even for a woman. He did. That's something. There might be more to him than you know, than he knows. Time he found out."

"But how can he help you?"

"There you'll have to trust me," he said

shortly. "Good night." He left her and cut back through the grove to his horse. She was a good woman, he decided, though vain and pampered, but he reserved trust on short acquaintance. On her relations with Hornbeck he made no judgment; it was no business of his. Though if Hornbeck felt guilty about merely meeting the woman, it was unlikely their affair had gone beyond a few almost decorous meetings.

Mounting up, McGivern kneed his horse into a trot, swinging in a roughly northeastern direction across the sweltering desert. He'd make night camp out there, and tomorrow set about establishing a permanent camp on some local promontory from which he could spot any effort to move the rifles from Chain Anchor. It should come soon, now that they knew he had definite knowledge of the gun cache.

He was sure that Belden would not carry on the actual trade, with a war party nearby. Each Apache warrior was his own man; even the tribal chief served only as a sort of senior counselor. On the warpath, an Apache made a grudging concession to the command of his war chiefs, but it was a thin check, and no sane white man would permit a whole band of blood-lusting Apaches on his ranch. Belden would do direct business with one or a few of the steadier heads of the party, and transport the rifles to an agreed rendezvous. Rifles in quantity would be conveyed only by wagon, and McGivern remembered the old wheel tracks he'd seen in the ridge canyon to the north. That was the place to watch; a weighted, slow-moving wagon would be easy to spot.

He raised his head, smelling the desert air; it held a rare, uneasy stir of air currents that he knew well: a storm, a bad one, was brewing. He'd have to choose this night's camp with an eye to good shelter.

He had already considered and rejected the idea of riding to Fort Laughlin and returning with a detachment of cavalry. Colonel Cahill would be swift to oblige on only McGivern's word, but the trip there and back would consume precious days, and during that time the guns could be moved, delivered, and the evidence gone. No, he'd wait and watch; when the guns moved out, he'd get another man and follow the gun wagon to rendezvous . . . and where could he find a more accredited witness than a lawman? That meant Sheriff Paul Hornbeck. McGivern thought grimly that Hornbeck would accompany him if he had to hogtie the sheriff. No matter how Hornbeck had blinded himself to Belden's machinations, he could not deny the plain evidence. With Mrs. Belden's persuasive help, Hornbeck's testimony would be secured at the proper time.

Their dual testimony would destroy Belden and future gun-running here, but what of the present shipment of rifles? McGivern knew that he must somehow prevent these guns from actually passing into Apache hands, and that would be the hardest trick of all to turn.

11

Reggie Harlan was in a temper when he finally ordered the men to break off the search and get back to the bunkhouse. As he stood in the ranchyard, hands on hips as he watched them disperse, his back and belly felt clammy with more than this day's furnace-like heat that had long since sweated him to irritability. *It had to be McGivern,* he thought sourly. *The damned Indian. We had him boxed, surrounded, and he slipped out. The Old Man'll be fit to be tied.*

He and Belden had been sure McGivern was responsible for the failure of Nachito or Maco or one of their men to show up at the ranch the day before yesterday, the date they'd set with Nachito a month ago, when the war chief had delivered the Army payroll chest to the ranch. That was in full payment for the first two hundred rifles Reggie had delivered to the Apaches four months earlier. Nachito was a man of his word. Besides, he'd been steadily gathering more reservation breakaways into his band, which he planned to build to army size with mixed youthful hotbloods from all six Apache tribes. He would need many more rifles — and the Army would send out more payroll trains.

McGivern was the fly in the ointment.

Reggie's suspicions of the man had crystallized two days ago when he'd lost McGivern on the road to Chain Anchor after talking to Lafe Elberg; the failure of the Apache agent to show up on that same day — for Nachito was always dependable — could be logically traced to his running head on into McGivern. This morning Reggie had ridden to the ridge canyon and traced it from one end to the other for telltale spoor; here and there the ground had been recently disturbed and all definite sign carefully obliterated, not enough left to follow up. Then today, those fools Kruger and Mills had let McGivern give them the slip.

McGivern was clever and thorough, and now he'd entered the ranch unseen, got into the barn between the guard change, found the cache, and killed Pride Bloom. Pride was a negligible loss. But McGivern's interest in what was going on was certain now, and the question was — what would he do next?

Reggie's hand shifted on his hip, touched the bone-handled knife he'd found by the torn-open gun crate in the loft. McGivern's. He drew it from his belt, turned it in his hands with the wry thought that he'd rather have the man. It was small comfort to know that McGivern could make a mistake like any other man.

Wearily Harlan pivoted on his heel and tramped up to the house, across the wide veranda, through the propped-open door into the parlor. Belden's flaccid bulk was stretched like a jellied mass on the leather divan. His shirt collar was open, his tie loose, and he was fanning himself with a folded newspaper. Opalescent drops of sweat shone on his oily moon face.

"Well, Reggie; and what luck?"

"None," Reggie growled as he pulled a straight-backed chair around, straddled it, and leaned his arms on the backrest. He glanced at the open book that lay face down on Belden's mounded stomach — *The Prince*, Machiavelli's classic study of dictatorship. Reggie had once begun it himself, only to toss it aside when he found there was nothing in it applicable to his wants. It was Belden's meat, though; man-of-power sort of thing. Money and prestige were fine, Reggie thought, for what they could get you — liquor, women, good times — but as an end in themselves, why bother?

"You fool," Belden wheezed softly. "Did he get into the barn?"

"He did, and into a gun crate. Killed Pride Bloom when Pride found him . . . and left his calling card." Reggie handed him the knife. "Must have dropped it. . . ."

"Why, this is fine," Belden said dryly, dropping the knife on the floor after a glance at it. Faint lights coalesced in his icy eyes. "It was McGivern, of course — and what will he do now?"

Reggie shrugged. There was a wintry silence which Reggie uneasily broke. "What about the rest of the gun shipment? You said the wagons from N'Orleans finally got here today."

Belden nodded coldly. "You'll send Kruger and Mills to bring them from the warehouse to the ranch tomorrow. Since I'm surrounded by incompetents, they're as good as any."

"The whole shipment'll be ready then," Reggie mused, "and still no word from Nachito."

"He's probably cautious — since his other man failed to return. The question is —" Belden's snappish tone broke off at a light sound of feet ascending the veranda. Lissa came in, riding crop in hand, her face a lovely mask.

"What do you mean," Belden wheezed, "riding out, with a prowler around?"

"Don't shout at the stars, George; they can't hear you."

"Ah," Belden murmured, "but you're somewhat more attainable than the cold and distant stars — eh, my dear?"

She flushed, bit back an angry retort, walked swiftly from the room down a corridor branching into one of the wings. A door banged behind her.

"Hornbeck," Belden murmured. "He left only a few minutes before the excitement — and Lissa went to her room for her riding togs."

"What do you care?" Reggie asked dryly.

"Ha ha ha," Belden said. "I don't, that's the beauty of it."

"You better let up on her. Innuendoes can rub hard, and you want to keep her happy."

"Let them rub the stupid wench," Belden said flatly. "Nobody knows Melissa better than I. The pleasures of a luxurious existence will more than balance the scales."

Reggie thought with quiet hate, *one of these days, Jumbo, you'll make a wrong judgment about someone in that cold, fishy way, and it'll kick back on you.* He swung his glance idly from Belden and it froze on the doorway to the big dining room, darkened now. He made out the hulking shadow of a man standing there in utter silence.

"What is it?" Belden demanded.

The shadow advanced noiselessly into the parlor and became a squat bull of a man, not tall, with short legs and abnormally long arms. His copper-hued face was flat-featured and bigoted, distorted by a great scar which twisted transversely from his left lower eyelid across his broad nose, cutting deeply into his upper lip and pulling it into a cruel grimace. His shoulder-length black hair was partly confined by a greasy warband, and he wore cotton pants stuffed into knee-length moccasins. A filthy calico shirt strained across his barrel chest; over it he wore a faded blue Army officer's tunic with one epaulette and all the buttons missing. An old cap-and-ball dragoon pistol was shoved in the trousers' waist.

Reggie had seen this Apache only once before, when he'd delivered the first shipment of guns to the rendezvous, but even a white man who thought all Indians looked alike could never forget this one. He had a chill sensation of wondering how long the fellow had been standing in the dining room — watching and listening.

"This is Maco," he told Belden.

The fat man wheezed himself up on his elbows, staring with interest at the co-leader of the Apache raiders. "Welcome, sir; we've been waiting on you. Reggie — your chair for the gentleman."

Maco grunted his contempt and squatted down a few feet from the divan. He stared with impassive fascination at Belden's obese hugeness before saying gutturally: "Where guns?"

Harlan hesitated before replying. Heretofore he had done business directly with Nachito or his lieutenant, Tah-zay. These two were the soul of honor, the half-Apache wrangler who worked for Chain Anchor had told Harlan when he'd first quizzed the man. The same wrangler had put Harlan in touch with some relatives at San Carlos, and through them arranged a meeting with Nachito. Nachito would always deliver full payment for the guns, would risk his life to keep his given word. How far could Maco be trusted?

"Nachito couldn't make it, eh?" Harlan said uneasily.

Maco's lip curled in undisguised contempt. "Nachito say not worry, you get money. Where guns?"

"Ready to go," Reggie said. "Only we might have to hold 'em up a while. . . ." Quietly, briefly, he explained the situation to the war chief. At mention of McGivern's name, he saw Maco start, mutter, *"Day-zen!"* and a glint of stark hatred fill the narrow eyes. It meant nothing to Reggie, and he went on, finishing: "You understand how it is."

"Enju. When get guns?"

"Ask him why Nachito or his man didn't show up two days ago," Belden put in.

"Him come back camp, bad hurt. Say only that white man shoot him; he not want talk. So Maco come through white man *hacienda* at back, listen. Think maybe white man goddamn liar, make doublecross Apache."

"And now you know differently, eh, Maco?" Belden smiled urbanely.

"When get guns?"

Belden scowled. "We can't move till we're sure it's safe. Listen, Maco; bring your people to rendezvous, and wait. We'll show up in a week at the outside."

Maco rose in a fluid movement, setting a hand to his knife hilt. "Fat *pinda-likoye,* voice like burro but smooth tongue like snake. Make trap, Maco come back, cut through fat to your heart. *Sabe?"*

"Ha ha ha," Belden said. "Perfectly. It's agreed, then."

Without another word, Maco glided to the doorway, vanished through it and was swallowed by the night.

Belden mopped his forehead with a silk handkerchief. "That's settled. Double the guards over those guns. That McGivern's Injun enough to come back, catch us off-guard and wreck them."

"Assume he's working for the Army," Reggie said. "Now he's got the guns spotted, won't he leave to fetch the soldiers, give us a chance to move the guns out?"

"I think not. Fort Laughlin is the closest Army outpost, several days' ride. He'd know we could move the guns in his absence, and then where would his evidence be? No — McGivern will stay to watch us."

"He might send someone for the Army, then."

"From *my* town? Come now . . ."

"He's friendly with Ma Gates," Reggie insisted. "That old bat's not afraid of us by a damn sight — and she's got people working for her."

"Very well. Station some men to watch her place and its employees. Get the rest of the crew out scouring the local range. Hunt McGivern down. *Get him.*"

"Easier said than done," Reggie said wryly.

"See to it, or it'll be your hide," Belden said flatly. As an afterthought, he added, "Get that fool Pride under the ground and out of the way."

Reggie nodded and left the house. On the veranda he paused to roll a cigarette, his mind a cold welter of hatred for the fat man. *Well, you're still footloose; you can always drift. But not,* he told himself, *till you've cut a bug hunk out of either*

George's profits or his fat carcass.

He bent his head to light the cigarette, then raised it sharply, listening . . . A horseman was swinging across the ranchyard from the town road. As he cantered into the soft spill of lamplight from the front windows, Reggie, with a start of surprise, recognized Clyde Prentiss. He stepped awkwardly down at the tie rail. Reggie saw that his hands were shaking, his shirt wilted with perspiration. His eyes jumped nervously. "I've got to see Mr. Belden."

Reggie waved a hand at the open door and followed Clyde inside. Curiously amused, Harlan took a position leaning against the doorjamb. He watched Clyde hesitate before approaching the divan where the fat man reclined.

"Yes, Clyde?" Belden said unconcernedly, not even glancing at the bookkeeper's paste-colored face.

Clyde's words poured out in a nervous rush. As he listened, Reggie's bored smile thinned, vanished. He straightened, his muscles tensing. Belden merely grunted, continuing to fan himself with the newspaper. When Clyde had finished, he glanced up at the bookkeeper, his murmur benevolent. "How much money do you want, Clyde?"

Clyde moistened his lips, his voice thin and high-pitched. "How much is my silence worth to you, sir?"

"Come, come, Clyde," Belden said jovially. "A good blackmailer calls his own shots. By the way," he added casually, "you hid the books in a safe place, of course, after examining them; presumably in the care of one or more people who knew you were coming here tonight."

"Why-why —" Prentiss' stammer, his vacant-eyed nervousness, gave him away.

"You didn't," Belden purred. "Of course anyone you confided in would want a cut of whatever you get out of me. But I'm very much afraid, my boy, that —" The divan creaked as he broke off speech and swung his bulk to a sitting position, facing Clyde with malevolent, mountainous calm.

"Wait a minute!" Clyde's voice rose shrilly, edged with panic; and Reggie guessed that Prentiss's greed had overruled his rabbity, cautious ways, given him the false confidence to come here tonight — and that he was only now getting an inkling of his danger. "Julia Lanphere told me about the gun-running — she knows —"

"Your saloon chippy? Doss she know that you came here to blackmail me? I thought not. What could she do if something . . . happened to you? What proof can she offer? The word of a saloon singer against George Belden?" Belden's wattles stirred with his gentle shake of the head. "You poor, pathetic fool," he said softly. "You've stepped far out of your depth, trying your game with professionals."

Prentiss flung about with a thin groan and ducked for the doorway. With an easy movement, Reggie pulled his Colt and slammed the barrel against Clyde's temple. Clyde plunged to the floor and lay motionless on his face. Reggie's wicked glance lifted to Belden. "Now?"

"A moment," the fat man said. He stooped, picked the bone-handled knife off the floor where he'd dropped it and examined it thoughtfully. "McGivern has also been friendly with this singer — what's her name? — Lanphere. If we killed McGivern and he's working for the Army — we'd be in trouble. But if McGivern and Clyde fought over the girl, and McGivern were hunted down as a murderer, he'd be safely out of our way and no danger to us."

Reggie scowled. "McGivern kill Clyde? How do you figure that?"

"Ha ha ha. Why," Belden wheezed softly, "when Clyde is found with McGivern's knife stuck in him, what else can folks think?"

12

That night McGivern made camp in the lee of a shelving outcrop on Chain Anchor's north range. He rolled into his blankets and went to sleep with the first thin rumblings of thunder in his ears. He was awakened at midnight when the storm broke in a torrential downpour. Near-solid sheets of wind-borne rain lashed the ground. He pulled his blankets deeper against the inner wall of the outcrop. Making certain his bed was high enough to drain away ground water and spare him a soaking, he rolled back in the blankets, hat over his eyes to shut out the blinding flare of lightning, and went stoically back to sleep, despite the roar of storm.

He awoke in the gray and dismal pre-dawn and looked out at a dripping, mist-bound world. There was a chill in the air. His horse had been tethered just outside, in the lee of the rock, to escape the full fury of the storm, and now it rolled shivering to its feet. McGivern briskly rubbed down its matted, glistening hide. His clothes were clammy with the heavy moisture in the air, and the only way to keep warm was to move.

He saddled the sorrel, mounted and rode briskly away toward Saguaro. It should take him an hour to reach town, and he would still have time to get what he needed before the towns-people were awake and stirring. He needed food, a good-sized bundle of it, to cache up on Chain Anchor's north boundary ridge; there might be days of waiting before the gun wagons moved out.

When the sprawl of town took bleak, vague shape out of the fog, he slackened his pace because of an inner caution. He had the cold conviction that after last night he would be hunted from one end of the range to the other by Belden's hardcases. Not that this greatly concerned him; he had foraged in the heart of Apache country and eluded the grim, canny warriors of Delgadito, Sal Juan, and Geronimo. Like the Apaches, he had found the plains and desert his natural element, as some men found theirs on the high seas. He'd never felt quite at ease in towns. After taking up residence in Silver City he'd often made long, lonely camping trips.

As he neared the buildings, they made a drab and cheerless prospect: it was a town full of enemies. His only friends there were Ma Gates and Julia Lanphere. Two friends, both women; they couldn't help. They might be closely watched from now on, and his own position would be dangerous enough without embroiling them.

He reined in at the southern outskirts beyond a hedgerow of cottonwoods, picking out the general store at the middle of the main block.

He'd swing back of the buildings and come up on the rear of the general store. It would be a simple matter to force the back-door lock, enter the storeroom, take his wants and leave payment. He rode in close behind the first building; reaching its far corner, he started to knee the animal on past the alleyway that separated it from the adjoining saloon.

Suddenly a cracked and quavering voice halted him with its unsteady warning: "Hold it there, mister."

McGivern turned slowly in his saddle, holding the reins high in his hands, careful to make no move that might be misinterpreted. An old man whose shrunken frame was muffled in an oversized slicker hobbled from the alley, a shotgun leveled shakily in his veined hands.

"Easy, Pop," McGivern counseled quietly. "That thing could cut a man in two."

The old man halted a few careful feet beyond McGivern's stirruped foot. "You damned murderin' skunk, I'd like nothing better," he husked in the same unsteady timbre. "Pile off, slow and on this side." The shotgun muzzle moved in a menacing semicircle.

McGivern swung stiffly down, threw his reins and faced the old man. "What is this?"

"You can pester the sheriff with your questions," snarled the old man. His head was bare above his glistening slicker, thin gray hair matted wetly to his angular skull. "He don't listen, the jedge will. Move!"

He stepped carefully aside, motioning with the shotgun at the alleyway. McGivern started down it, and the old man fell in behind. When they reached the street, the oldster said tersely, "Stop here." He faced the north end of town, raising his voice in a shrill yell: "Paul! Paul, I got him! Come a-hyperin'!"

A stocky figure emerged from an alley at the far end of the street and legged it toward them, a slicker flapping about its legs. *Hornbeck,* McGivern thought. *He and the old man were waiting for me to show up. Whatever this is, it's serious. Watch yourself.*

The sheriff hauled up breathlessly in front of them. His face was flushed with a kind of vindictive righteousness; his glistening slicker arms lifted and pointed a Greener at McGivern's stomach. "I knew you'd show up if I waited long enough. You had to come back — to get grub, or to see that saloon slut. Don't say anything, McGivern; don't even breathe hard. Just walk. The jail's on your right."

McGivern tramped toward the sheriff's office, the cold fury in him dampened by the threat of the two shotguns. Either man would be glad of a chance to use them. He entered the office, a bare room whose brick walls were almost solidly papered with reward dodgers. He stood with Hornbeck's weapon targeting him while the old man skirted the rolltop desk and lifted a ring of keys from a wall peg. He unlocked the corridor door to the cell block and stood aside while

131

Hornbeck nudged McGivern through. They halted before an end cell, and McGivern stepped inside. The door rang shut with an echo of finality, and the old man turned the key.

McGivern gripped the bars tight in an effort to hold his voice steady. "You want to tell me about this, Sheriff?"

"Is it anything you don't know?" Hornbeck asked sardonically.

"So far you haven't said a damned thing. If that tin star makes you holier-than-thou, it also gives me a right or so, like hearing why I'm charged."

"I don't need the law read to me by your likes," Hornbeck said glacially. "All right, keep your little pose. About four hours ago Clyde Prentiss was found over by the creek — knifed to death."

McGivern's stomach recoiled as from an icy sledgehammer blow; he said slowly, "You in the habit of nailing a stranger for murder because he's convenient?"

With a smug, bitter smile, Hornbeck unbuttoned his slicker, reached in an inside pocket and brought out a handkerchief-wrapped object. He opened it in his palm, and McGivern saw the knife he'd left in Chain Anchor's barn loft last night — the knife with an oddly designed bone haft he'd carved himself, the razor-edged blade honed from an old file and now covered with rusty stains.

"Yours, isn't it?"

"That's for you to find out," McGivern said, his face impassive as stone.

"I already questioned the girl. She identified the knife as yours."

"Julia Lanphere, you mean?"

"That's the slut."

"Hornbeck," McGivern said softly, "use that word again —"

"And you'll tear down the bars to reach me?" Hornbeck's lip curled. "You arrogant, uncivilized desert rats are all alike . . . crowing your mockery of society and its laws even after you're caged. The girl was seen often with you or Prentiss. It's obvious . . . a jealous quarrel. The two of you go off from town a ways to settle it. Prentiss is unarmed, no match for a brute like you. One thrust to the heart is all that's needed."

"And the knife left for you to find."

"Panic, sure. Why not? Your kind is all bluff and bluster. You can kick a man silly in a dirty saloon brawl, but murder is something else. You struck in anger — then lost your head and ran." Hornbeck's thick fist closed around the handkerchief and knife. "You're sewed up, McGivern. Your confession will save us both time and trouble — because I mean to sweat one out of you."

McGivern disciplined his wild-running thoughts, steadied his voice. "Sheriff," he said mildly, "Miss Lanphere told you about the knife. Did she also explain our relationship?"

Hornbeck frowned. "Gave me a lengthy cock-

and-bull story about your working for the Army, trying to locate guns that Mr. Belden, of all people, is smuggling to the Apaches. That Clyde Prentiss was trying to help, and must have been found out — and murdered by Mr. Belden."

"It didn't strike that logical mind of yours that the story was a shade involved to be made up on short notice."

"It was made up," Hornbeck said grimly, "but not by her. *You.* You told her that to make yourself a hero in her eyes, turn her attention from Prentiss to yourself."

"Look —" McGivern masked his desperation with quiet-toned patience — "you can check my story with Colonel Cahill — Fort Laughlin."

"Sonny," the old jailer jeered, "don't you fret none; he will."

"But it'll take days by letter, and Saguaro has no telegraph. By that time. . . . Listen to me, Sheriff."

"I've listened to enough damned slander about the town's foremost citizen," Hornbeck shouted.

"One question, inside my rights. Who found Prentiss' body . . . in the middle of the night?"

"One of the Chain Anchor hands — Kruger by name," Hornbeck snapped. "It was just after the storm ended. He came to rouse me out, took me to the spot. We brought the body to Doc Beeman's — he's the coroner — and had the knife removed. Then I went to question the

Lanphere girl, and afterward stationed myself and my deputy at opposite ends of town to wait for you. I counted on your desert rat's gall, not your guts, to bring you back."

"The coroner found no other marks on the body?"

Hornbeck scowled, shrugged curtly. "A bruise on the temple — doubtless made when Prentiss fell with your knife in him."

"And Kruger, one of Belden's hands, happened to be drifting down by the creek in the middle of the night and discovered the body."

"McGivern," Hornbeck said in an edged voice, "one more! One more inference about Mr. Belden and I'll open this cell —"

"And work me over with a bottle?" McGivern jeered softly, thinking, *if I could rawhide him close enough to grab that Greener.* . . . He went on cuttingly, "I hear that's how you work best, bottle in your hand."

Abruptly Hornbeck calmed. He pointed a finger, shaking it gently. "All right, McGivern. I can wait. To watch you swing. Laugh yourself blue in the face while you think about it." To the old jailer he said curtly, "Come on, Eph," and the two tramped down the corridor.

The cell door closed and McGivern sank onto the edge of the narrow cot, a slow, cold despair settling to his marrow. He felt a swift flare of anger at Julia Lanphere, but it died as quickly. It had been his own fault for trusting a woman. Yet that wasn't right; she had tried to enlist help sensibly . . . through Clyde Prentiss, who alone was in a position to collate material that might smash Belden, with no personal risk. But Prentiss had been careless or unlucky; McGivern's knife in his body, plus the fact that Julia had been seen with both men, would add up to a jealous quarrel. Even a fair-minded lawman would be obliged to think as Hornbeck had; the inquest would lead to a murder trial.

From time to time McGivern had sent Colonel Cahill reports on the progress of his long quest, but even if the colonel produced those letters, the scales would balance toward the scaffold. If Belden had had McGivern murdered, the colonel could have turned McGivern's reports over to the U.S. Marshal; there would be dangerous investigations by government agents. Successfully framing McGivern for murder would discredit those reports; only Cahill and McGivern would know the truth — truth that would die with McGivern, and leave the colonel helpless.

From the street, McGivern heard a familiar sound that brought him to the high, barred window facing an alley. Squeezing his face to the bars, he brought his angle of vision to the patch of street showing between the jail and the adjacent building. A wagon was creaking past, from the direction of Belden's freight yards toward the south road, and on the seat he caught a glimpse of Kruger and Mills. The small load in the wagon bed was tarp-covered. That would be the last of the guns for the present quota, on

136

their way to join the others.

Voices in the outer office brought him back to the cell door, straining his ears. He recognized Reggie Harlan's amiable, deep-chested drawl. "So he's caught. I was going to send the crew out to help run him down, but this saves us trouble. Good work, Sheriff. It's news that'll please Mr. Belden. Got to keep this town clean of such murdering riffraff."

"It's my job," was Hornbeck's reply, but his voice held a note of obvious pleasure.

Because Mr. Belden will be pleased, McGivern thought with weary irony — and he guessed that inside an hour, when Belden was informed that McGivern was safely in jail, the completed shipment of guns would be on its way to the Apaches.

Restlessly he paced the cell, hardly hearing the door close behind Harlan and then Hornbeck saying magnanimously, "You've been up half the night, Eph; go home and get some sleep . . . Oh, you might take McGivern's horse to the stable; and put his keep on the county bill."

"Yessir, Paul; thankee."

An hour and more passed, and then McGivern lost track of time. Along the savage run of his thoughts, his mind trailed up a dozen false spoors and backtracked relentlessly to a solitary checkmate of all Belden's moves: he had to escape and follow his original plan — to track down and destroy the guns. But he had an additional reason for needing an accompanying witness only by seeing the evidence of Belden's gun-running would Hornbeck be persuaded that Belden had framed McGivern for Prentiss' murder.

He halted in the middle of his cell, turning slowly to scan it for the twentieth time. The jail had been built to last; the floors were of solid oak, the walls of tightly mortared fieldstone. He fisted the barred door in both hands, braced his body and shook it. The lock rattled faintly; that was all. The door was anchored to an oak frame by three deep-sunk bolts in each hinge. Even with a prying or bolting tool, he'd be discovered long before he could remove the door, and there would still be the cellblock door and Hornbeck or his jailer to get past. McGivern flung himself on his back across the cot, a hand rubbing his aching eyes. Hopeless. It was hopeless. . . .

Another familiar voice brought him back to his feet, his heart pounding. It was Ma Gates' raucous tones flailing Hornbeck out in the office.

"I don't care what you think," Hornbeck shouted exasperatedly. "I have plenty of evidence to hold him. Anyway I don't know how you heard."

"That mouthy mothbag of an Eph Johnson was shootin' his trap off over in the Belle Fourche not five minutes ago," Ma snapped back. "Now lemme lay down a law, knothead. One statin', to wit, that we get five minutes with a prisoner. Georgie and me aim to have 'em."

"Very well," Hornbeck said coldly, then after a moment's hesitation: "I can't very well search women, so I'll have to go with you. Leave your handbags on the desk."

Ma Gates gave a contemptuous snort. McGivern stepped back, sinking onto the cot as Ma and Julia Lanphere came in, followed by Hornbeck with a drawn Colt in one hand and a key ring in the other. Curtly motioning the women to stand away, he unlocked the cell door and stepped back to the far wall, keeping his gun out.

Julia was first inside, tall and statuesque in a dark blue dress that contrasted with the pallor of her face. Her usual poise was shaken by a frightened concern. "Tom," she said softly. "I'm sorry. I didn't mean this to happen. I tried to tell Hornbeck —"

"Forget it," he broke in quietly. "It's done."

She made a small, unhappy gesture, biting her lower lip. Ma Gates brushed past her, the cot squawking as she lowered her hefty bulk alongside McGivern. "So what can we do for you, Mac? Better name it now; your head's in a noose."

"Afraid the warbag's all sewed up, Ma — for now." He was astonished then to see the big woman sniffle, fumble inside the voluminous bosom of her black dress and bring out a handkerchief. She raised it to her nose and blew loudly. He knew at once that she was putting on an act; she'd come to help him, but how? For friendship's sake and to spite the law — and no doubt with some persuasion from Julia — Ma Gates, once she'd made her decision, would go all the way. He fell in with her pretense, saying gently, "Now, Ma."

Her hand came down and covered his at his side. "Aaaahh," she said, fashioning a husky note for Hornbeck's benefit, "You know me. Heart of stone."

"Sure."

"Just that you're a favorite of mine, always was, always will be. Even if you done it, poor boy." McGivern winced inwardly, thinking, *don't overplay it, Ma.*

She turned her hand then and let something hard and cold slip from the folded handkerchief against his hand. At the same time, Julia had moved a step sideways, her full skirt momentarily cutting between them and Hornbeck's intense and watchful gaze. The sheriff cleared his throat irritably, and Julia stepped away, a second after McGivern had jammed the object under his thigh, recognizing its shape and feel without looking down.

Ma stood with a brusque movement, one glinting eye fashioning a broad wink, on the side away from Hornbeck. "Need anything, you get word to Ma. Make a hell of a character witness, but anything else. . . ." Her majestic head turned toward Julia. "Got anything on your mind, girl, spill it."

140

"I'll just say again — I'm sorry, Tom." Her face and voice held a desperate plea for understanding that was not part of the act, and McGivern said gently, putting into it all the sincerity he dared, "It was enough, your coming here, Julia. You and Ma."

The women left the cell. Sitting tautly, McGivern listened to their waning footsteps, wanting to give them time to get clear. Hornbeck moved to the cell door and locked it. He turned away, sheathing his gun, and started back to the office.

McGivern heard the street door close behind Julia and Ma Gates. He moved swiftly and silently to the front of his cell and shoved his arm between the bars, rapping a sharp order: "Stop there, Sheriff. Get your hands up before you turn."

13

Hornbeck halted in his tracks, just ahead of the cellblock door, his broad back stiffening. Slowly his hands went up as he came around, blood mounting to his face; he stared at the derringer in McGivern's extended hand. "Come on," McGivern said harshly. "The keys. . . ."

Hornbeck tramped back to the cell, his face a study in frustrated wrath. McGivern drew his arm in, motioning at the lock. "Lower your left hand with the keys. That's all you'll need."

Hornbeck fumbled with the lock; as the key turned, McGivern pushed the door wide, and almost in the same motion scooped Hornbeck's Colt from its holster. With an ungentle hand he turned Hornbeck and shoved him against the wall, facing it. Swiftly he broke the loading gate of the Colt, shucked out the shells, jammed the empty gun in Hornbeck's holster. "Fast, now. You got handcuffs?"

"Left — hip pocket," Hornbeck said in a low, choked way.

McGivern lifted out the manacles and clamped one over his own right wrist, the other over Hornbeck's left. With a rough yank he turned Hornbeck to face him, slamming the derringer in his fisted left hand into Hornbeck's stomach. The sheriff grunted, doubling in a way that brought his face within three inches of McGivern's.

"Listen. I'll say it just once." McGivern's quiet voice held dead certainty. "We're walking out together, you and I. You'll keep your free hand resting on your gun, not forgetting it's empty. My hand'll be in my pocket, around this derringer. We'll go to the stables and pick up our horses. If anyone asks, you're taking me over to the creek where Prentiss' body was found; we're going to check for sign. That'll be the truth. And hear me. . . ." McGivern moved the derringer till the short muzzle jammed deep in Hornbeck's throat. The sheriff's Adam's apple moved convulsively. "One wrong word, one wrong move, and you're dead. Understand that. What's at stake is more important than your life or mine."

He swung away from Hornbeck, shoving the hand with the gun into the pocket of his buckskin jacket, then tugging the sheriff with him down the corridor, into the office. He paused long enough to get his gun and shell belt from Hornbeck's desk and buckle the belt under his jacket. They stepped out. The sky was still overcast, with a dreary nip to the air; a few people moved along the street, giving the two men only curious glances.

"The stable," McGivern murmured. "And keep your hand on your gun. You're being careful with me."

The boardwalk echoed solidly beneath their

feet as they tramped a full block to the livery. In spite of the chill, McGivern felt warm sweat gather along his back and belly; his eyes quested the street restlessly for sign of any of Belden's gunnies. Probably they had all been summoned in to help move the rifles.

The two men turned in at the livery archway, and the ancient hostler showed no curiosity at all as Hornbeck curtly ordered him to saddle their horses. McGivern stood tensely in the runway, watching the street, voicelessly cursing the hostler's infuriating slowness as he readied the horses. With a jerk on the handcuffs, McGivern signed Hornbeck to mount first; as the sheriff settled heavily into leather, Mc-Givern made a twisting leap that carried him astride the sorrel. Their mounts were crowded close because of the awkward length of chain fettering their wrists. McGivern kneed his horse into motion, and Hornbeck hesitated only a moment before following suit.

They rode slowly apace down south Main street, then turned right at the end of the block, hitting the cottonwood-bordered creek road where it wended southwest along the stream bed. The desert rolled flat as a griddlecake away from the low banks. The fog was dissipated now, but iron-gray still mantled the sky and laid its grim pallor across the land.

Hornbeck's voice, freighted with contempt, broke the silence. "I don't know what you hope to gain by this."

"You'll see. Just don't miss the place."

"Those women are accessories. They smuggled a gun to a killer. I'll see they're called to reckoning." Hornbeck's tone held a smug note of satisfaction.

He feels very righteous now, McGivern thought. *He's tied it all into one neat moral bundle.* A saloon proprietress and ex-madam, with the help of a honky-tonk slut, had manipulated the escape of a murderer. A cold resentment drove McGivern to say bitingly, "Your sense of respectability extend to other men's wives, Hornbeck?"

For a moment his outraged awareness that McGivern knew about Melissa Belden was stark in Hornbeck's face; then it sheathed with a protective aloofness. He said distantly, "What do you know of medieval times, McGivern — of knighthood?"

"Not a hell of a lot."

"Men of old extended their protection and affection to a lady in return for her favor. It was a mark of high breeding and courtliness. Nothing that you'd understand."

"Oh," McGivern said soberly, "it's crystal clear."

Hornbeck gave him a stony glance, then hunched his black-suited shoulders and grimly shut his mouth. McGivern wondered wryly whether the man was only a sounding board for the opinions and manners he'd heard. In the narrowly drawn lines of Hornbeck's thoughts, there were only "good" women or "bad" women

— never people who were women. Not even Mrs. Belden's condemnation of her husband could shake Hornbeck's black-and-white ruling that George Belden had raised him, a drunkard, from a social abyss of evil. Hornbeck had despised his fault, but had been too weak to change by himself: a good woman had helped; somehow he'd rationalized away the fact that the "good" woman wanted to run off with him, obviously a sin in Hornbeck's rule book. Still, he had changed outwardly, even to copying some solid citizen's neat, careful speech. And gave a prating of dead chivalric custom as an excuse for the only honest feeling he had, his love for Melissa Belden. Or was that too a self-imposed illusion, part of the man's total pose? Maybe the man was hopeless, McGivern thought despairingly, a useless pig in the poke for this desperate gamble . . . but it was too late to turn back.

"That's the place," Hornbeck had reined in, and McGivern checked the sorrel, following the sheriff's pointing finger to a small, willow-fringed swale at the water's edge. Awkwardly the two of them dismounted, left the horses with trailing reins and clambered down the bank. McGivern quickly read the story in the soft, trampled mud left by last night's rain.

He began to talk quietly, pointing out obvious signs to Hornbeck, who followed his explanation with surly reluctance. "There were two horses here, Sheriff. A man dismounted from

146

one, dragged something heavy and limp off the other — a body — carried it a few yards — see the double weight on the footprints — and dropped it . . . here. That where you found Prentiss?"

Hornbeck muttered an assent, his face intent now in spite of himself. "Man walked back to his horse and mounted," he continued. "Walloped the other horse into a run — let's say back toward Belden's ranch. Then he put his mount up the bank to the road, and — let's say again — went to town to fetch you. Here's where the two of you came down the bank to pick up Prentiss' body."

He turned to meet a hostile glare; Hornbeck said: "You could have left Prentiss here yourself — after you killed him."

McGivern nodded wearily. "You've seen I wear moccasins; this fellow had boots. Don't say I could have changed to boots; let it ride. Just remember what you see, that's all. No time to waste . . . The key to those cuffs." Hornbeck fumbled out the key and extended it. "Your pleasure," McGivern added, balancing his Colt in his left hand.

After Hornbeck had stowed the cuffs and key in his pocket, McGivern said, "Go ahead of me to your horse."

"Where to now — if you don't mind saying?"

"You had supper there last night."

"Chain Anchor? How far do you intend carrying this farce, McGivern?"

McGivern smiled faintly. "It's likely to be a long ride, Sheriff; a long, long ride. It's your duty though, and you get paid for it. I get nothing but satisfaction."

Hornbeck released a soft groan, facing McGivern with clenched fists.

"You heard me, Sheriff."

Hornbeck's stolid shape slogged up the muddy bank, and he mounted and fisted his reins with a furious resignation, waiting for McGivern to mount and motion him into the lead. They struck due east, swinging to give the town a wide berth on the south, and soon hit the Chain Anchor road. The murkiness was thinning at last and banked clouds rolled in, these in turn giving way to colorless sunlight hazily shafting their soft bellies. McGivern placed the position of the hidden sun, gauging the time as midmorning; there would be plenty of time to catch the slow-moving gun wagon.

When they achieved the mouth of the horse-shoe ridge that enclosed the ranch headquarters, McGivern cautiously slowed and ordered Hornbeck to ride a horse's length ahead. The whole layout appeared deserted, but a few of the crew might have remained. He rode slowly behind Hornbeck, his drawn gun lying ready against his thigh.

As they neared the gravel drive fronting the main house, the front door swung open. The first creak of hinges pulled McGivern to a halt, his gun lifting. He heard a raucous voice wheeze, "Lissa — come back! I'll shoot." Then Melissa Belden came running out, her face as white as her shirtwaist. She started across the yard, then wheeled with a little cry as George Belden's rotund form waddled out, a rifle in his hands. He halted with a startled grunt at sight of the two men, began to swing the rifle awkwardly up across his stomach.

McGivern fired from the hip. Shards of wood flew from the doorframe a foot from Belden's head. "Drop it," McGivern ordered.

Belden froze in mid-movement, glaring like some grotesque gargoyle, half-raised rifle pointed groundward. Slowly he unclenched his hands and the rifle clattered to the veranda. Melissa Belden let out an inheld breath, then turned and walked to Hornbeck's stirrup. "Paul, what is it? *What's happening?*"

Hornbeck had been watching Belden; now his dumbfounded stare lowered to her, speechlessly. McGivern kneed his horse to the tie rail and stepped down. He walked up to Belden, slapped his clothes for concealed weapons, then said sharply, "Come over here, Mrs. Belden. Tell me what happened."

Melissa came back to the veranda, followed by Hornbeck. The sheriff's face was a bewildered study at what he was seeing and hearing. Melissa told them, a stiff automatic quality to her words, that she usually slept late, that this morning a noise had awakened her. She had thrown on a wrap and come outside, to see her husband, Harlan, and the crew over by the barn. The crew were loading oblong-shaped boxes onto a freight wagon. She'd been puzzled, but then Harlan had turned and seen her, and his look had been frightening. She had hurried inside.

Shortly Belden had come in and told her to forget what she had seen. She had known something was wrong, and then she'd remembered how McGivern had come to the ranch the night before and knew that his coming had something to do with this secrecy. Belden had read her thought in her face; he'd twisted her arm and forced out of her how she had helped McGivern escape. She swore she knew nothing else, and it left him undecided. Soon the wagon had rolled, accompanied by the entire crew, and all the while since her husband had plied her with questions she could not answer.

"McGivern," she pleaded, "please — will you tell me what this is all about?"

"What I tried to tell Hornbeck here," McGivern said tersely, grimly. "Your husband is running guns to hostile Apaches."

Hornbeck raised one hand in a gestured plea. "George, you're not denying it!"

Belden's toadlike gaze held a fathomless contempt.

"He knows better than to say anything," McGivern said softly, "before he sees his lawyer. Nothing I have so far would stand in a court of law, and he knows it. Now I'll say why I brought

150

you with me, Sheriff. You and I are following that wagon. You're going to see the proof with your own eyes."

Hornbeck's expression was vacant and stunned. "It can't be true."

"It *is* true, Paul!" Melissa said passionately. "It's got to be." She caught him by the arms, almost shaking him. "You didn't believe me before — about George. This isn't just hearsay, this will *prove* it!"

Hornbeck said dully, "Is there something between you and McGivern?"

"Paul, for the love of heaven —"

"Hornbeck," McGivern cut in coldly and positively, "there's no time to argue with you." He tilted up his gun a half inch. "You're coming if I have to buffalo you and tie you across your saddle."

Slowly and doggedly Hornbeck shook his head. "No. I can't. This could ruin everything. It will. No, not that."

"Ah, that's it," Melissa breathed. "George gave you a comfortable little niche of status. You can't stand on your feet without it. You'd rather live out your life under a shoddy pretense."

Hornbeck shrugged dully. "This badge was supposed to mean something. What does it mean now, Lissa?"

"Whatever meaning you give it!" she said vehemently. "No more, no less. If George pinned it on you to serve his own ends and you let him have his way, you'll prove yourself to be exactly what he thought you were . . . a weakling who can be twisted for anyone's purpose, but never your own. Oh, Paul, there's a limit to how far anybody can help you, even me. You've got to help yourself!"

McGivern spoke with a flat edge of impatience. "Say how it's to be, Hornbeck. Now."

"Yes, Paul, decide." Melissa's face was filled with angry color. "You can go with McGivern the hard way . . . or make your choice now, for yourself. Else you've seen me for the last time."

"Not that, Lissa," he said weakly.

"That. I'm leaving George. I can leave you as easily." Her voice faltered slightly, then strengthened. "I can, Paul."

Belden started to chuckle, his vast gut trembling. He made no sound, yet the chuckle mounted to a noiseless, mirthless laugh. Melissa turned on him, her voice low and hate-filled. "Stop it, George, stop it."

Hornbeck looked up; his eyes focused, narrowed down. "Don't do that, George." McGivern wisely held his tongue, watching the slow, crazed anger fill Hornbeck's face. "Pious Paul," Belden wheezed between chortles. "Pious Paul and lovely, luxury-struck Melissa. I give you much joy of each other."

Something ugly and warped behind the fat man's Olympian benevolence was naked, and the sight of it seemed to snap whatever cowed fantasy Hornbeck held about the man. He lunged between McGivern and Lissa, his long fingers fastening around Belden's throat. His lunge sent them both stumbling back through the open door, Belden's weight crashing to the parlor floor with an impact that shook the house.

Hornbeck was on him, thick hands choking the laugh to a gurgle. Belden's eyes popped fishlike in his skull, a last breath clawing noisily from his throat before the deepening force of Hornbeck's fingers pinched off his wind. His small, womanish hands pulled futilely at Hornbeck's wrists. The tide of red that filled his jowls shaded to a swollen purple.

McGivern watched, his gun hanging loosely fisted at his side, a faint, grim smile on his lips. "Oh, stop it!" Lissa cried. "Stop it!"

McGivern took two steps and closed his hand on Hornbeck's shoulder. "That's enough."

Hornbeck seemed not to hear. When McGivern tried to pull him off, his stocky body was rigid with unleashed fury. McGivern whipped his Colt up and down in a short, chopping arc that ended against Hornbeck's temple. He caught the sheriff's limp weight and supported him to a leather divan.

Hornbeck sat up with a grimace of pain as Melissa came over, kneeling at his side with eyes full of compassion. He looked at her stupidly, then at McGivern. "You hit me."

"After you'd proved your point."

"By God," Hornbeck muttered, ducking his head and gingerly rubbing it. He looked up again. "By God."

153

"Feels that way, doesn't it?" McGivern smiled faintly. "Can you ride?"

A kind of surprised intelligence mingled with a half-baffled exultance filled Hornbeck's long face. His eyes met McGivern's with a level regard. "Any time."

14

They got Belden into his room and handcuffed him to the iron bedstead. The fat man was wheezing like a fish out of water, still unable to speak when Hornbeck and McGivern left him asprawl the bed and went out to their horses.

Melissa stepped onto the veranda, her eyes troubled as she watched them mount. "Paul," she said then, "I — I want to go with you. There's nothing for me here."

"I'll be back, Lissa."

"If you don't come back?" It left her like a lost cry.

"I'll be back." He frowned, holding in his fiddlefooting horse. "It'll be dangerous enough without a woman. You'll be all right here . . . George can't hurt you now. It has to be this way." He looked at McGivern for confirmation. The scout nodded. Melissa said nothing. She watched in silence as they rode from the ranch-yard.

McGivern wordlessly led the way, cutting north from the ranch along the fresh-rutted wheel tracks. Harlan and the others had a broad start, but even so they'd make slow time with the heavily loaded wagon. Once the pursuers were close it would be simple to trail them at a distance to the rendezvous. What happened afterward would be the difficult and dangerous part . . .

Hornbeck rode jauntily, shoulders squared against his horse's rocking gait, and McGivern knew that the man had found himself with a vengeance. Heady wine for a man in his mid-thirties who had spent half a lifetime leaning on outward props — whisky and then false prestige and a woman's sympathy — rather than find strength in the hard, independent core of himself. McGivern wondered if Hornbeck was only caught up in a reaction of extreme bravado after a cowed lifetime. He considered that carefully and decided that the man's self-finding was real; he'd only needed the sudden triggering of Belden's mockery to release it. The reaction might still leave him over-confident for a while, overbalanced to rashness; the business facing them called for cool thinking and steady hands. *Cross that bridge when it comes up,* McGivern thought then. He bent his full attention to the trail.

There was a thrum of hoofbeats from behind, which McGivern was the first to hear. He reined in and quartered his animal around facing their backtrail. Hornbeck ranged over beside him, squinting against the sun. Then the sheriff blurted, "It's Lissa."

"Not surprising," McGivern said shortly, "is it?"

She pulled to a halt, flushed and a little

breathless. She had changed to rough trousers and a man's hickory shirt, her rich auburn hair topped by a floppy hat. A breath of wind toiled with and loosened a few wisps of hair across her face, and she pushed them back with a hand, the gesture oddly defiant, as was the strong determination in her face.

She touched a bulging knapsack slung from her saddlehorn. "You'll need food and water. I've brought both."

"We'd have made out, but thank you nonetheless," McGivern said with elaborate dryness. "I see you also brought yourself dressed for a trip. It's no go, Mrs. Belden."

Her chin lifted. "Yes? And why not?" Her eyes softened a little, looking at Hornbeck. "I'm going with you, Paul. If you don't come back, neither do I. It's that simple. There's nothing else I can do."

A harried anger stirred in Hornbeck's face. "Listen, Melissa . . ." His voice trailed off helplessly. "McGivern, can't you say something?"

"Nothing I haven't said . . . and nothing I didn't mean."

"You're overlooking a practical point, Mr. McGivern," she observed flatly. "The more witnesses to this, the better. Particularly when — when one or more may not return alive."

"A woman can't testify against her husband, and I'm after Belden's scalp — his alone."

The defiance drained from her face, to be replaced by a softened, begging plea. "You're a

157

hard, self-sufficient man, but you must understand . . . a little. Didn't you ever care for someone enough that — that everything else came second in your life?"

McGivern's hand fisted on his lifted reins. Her words had broken through his defense; and he knew by the wondering triumph in her expression that she had seen it. "Once," he said in a tight undertone.

Melissa seized on it with a woman's intuitive accuracy. "A girl. Did something happen to her?"

"Yes."

"You were there?"

He shook his head in negation, then avoided her eyes.

"Didn't you wish that you could have shared . . . what happened?"

"Mrs. Belden —"

"You understand that much, then," she said softly. "It's worse for a woman. A man who loses his woman still has his work — his ambitions — his life interests. Or revenge, if nothing else." He winced faintly. She said then: "A woman who loses, loses everything. I can't lose him and go on alone, not when there's this last chance for us both. That's why I'm coming."

"Melissa," Hornbeck said humbly.

"I won't be in your way. I may even be of some help."

"That's not likely," McGivern said roughly, to cover his feelings; a curt jerk of his head motioned her to fall in behind, ignoring the half-angry, half-sheepish reproach in Hornbeck's face.

At high noon they halted deep on Chain Anchor's north range, just short of the barrier ridge, to rest and eat. Melissa had packed a practical grubsack of staples ideal for a dry and fireless camp. Since it would probably be bite-and-run later, McGivern warned them to eat their fill and get some rest afterward.

By midafternoon they had penetrated to the end of the canyon bisecting the ridge and were on the sterile and waterless wastes to the north. From the flats with which McGivern had become familiarized by previous excursions, the land rose to a semi-plateau which rolled limitlessly to the north and east, desolate and broken irregularly by massive lava formations. Only a few twisted, scraggly juniper and piñon were lodged in the shattered, tortured rocks that reared like menacing sentries on every side of the wagon trail straggling between them over hard-baked clay levels. The trail was the only sign of white man's invasion of this wild country, which still belonged to the buzzard, the snake, and roaming bands of renegade Apaches. The broiling sun slanting ruthlessly against their backs began its slow sapping of the strength of Hornbeck and the woman; McGivern had to caution them to conserve their water.

Because McGivern had deliberately held a slow pace to spare the horses and keep a careful distance between them and the wagon and its armed guards, it was late afternoon before the wagon hove briefly into view, then jolted again out of sight behind a rocky shoulder. Hornbeck and Melissa, drooping with heat exhaustion, failed to notice anything, and McGivern said nothing. Harlan had no suspicion he was being followed; to his knowledge McGivern was safely jailed. It accounted for his confident failure to put out flankers or a rear guard.

The land became higher and more rugged. This was not mountain country, but McGivern suspected they were mounting the lower spine of a northern range where it petered out. That would account for the heightening, choppy aspect of the terrain. He guessed the rendezvous would be deep in the heart of this area. It was ideal: accessible even to a heavy wagon, but remote and rugged enough to throw off an unskilled tracker. Already the clay floor of the plateau had thinned away to broken, treacherous shale, and McGivern had to dismount frequently to check sign. Sometimes it was the work of minutes to discover even a fragment of shale freshly clipped by a shod hoof, or a rare horse dropping. Several times he lost sign altogether and had to work the backtrail patiently in a concentric circle to find where the wagon had made a sudden turn.

At last they rode over a humped jag of creosote and saw the distant wagon entering a rounded, saddle-shaped break in a gigantic serrated hogback. McGivern motioned the others swiftly back behind the creosote. That hogback must be the atrophied spine of this high terrain, and on its other side the land would fall away again. *Close to rendezvous now*, he hazarded. That was why he wanted to hold to shelter for a few minutes. The Apaches could have sentinels on that ridge, watching for the wagon, and its arrival would bring them down. *It better*, he thought.

He squeezed the sorrel into motion, some of his excitement communicated to the animal; it pricked its ear and fiddlefooted foolishly as he put it across the creosote hump. Hornbeck and Melissa fell in with his lead without words, and he knew that they too, alerted by his sudden halt, had seen the wagon.

In fifteen minutes they reached the saddle. McGivern took swift note of a narrow niche cleaving the ridge wall, barely wide enough for one horseman to enter at a time. It afforded concealment beneath the beetling upper ramparts of the ridge. He ordered Melissa and the sheriff to head their horses into it and await his return.

"What'll you do?" Hornbeck asked quickly.

"Go over that saddle on foot. See the other side."

"Alone?"

"Mister," McGivern said patiently, "you're in hostile country. Your enemy's the sharpest, toughest desert fighter alive. I told you before, your life or mine don't matter. We just have to stay alive long enough to spike the enemy's guns. That means scouting the layout by someone who can meet an Apache on his home ground, and that means me. You'd be in the way. Lie low and keep quiet."

Without waiting for a reply, he slid to the ground with his pair of Army fieldglasses in hand, turning his horse into the niche with a slap on the rump. At an easy, low-bent lope he entered the saddle dip without looking back. The trail sloped up for a good hundred yards, and then downward at a treacherous angle. McGivern now found himself looking across a limitless plain that hazed into the far horizon, and the sight brought him to a surprised standstill. Instead of the gentle tapering-off of the heights he'd expected, the far side of the ridge dropped sharply. The incline was fairly gentle up here, but soon it sheered off in a steep drop hundreds of feet to a slow-crawling river at its base, heavily silted to a murky yellow.

Moving on a few yards, he lowered himself to his belly and lay in watchful immobility. The majestic pitch of the wall below was broken only by an occasional flat ledge of tilted shale. One such ledge protruded from the gentler upper incline, and toward this the wagon was careering and jolting. The hoorawing of the driver, the squeal of brake shoes, drifted up. It was a tricky negotiation, but the driver expertly achieved the ledge and hauled up the team.

The horsemen crowded around the wagon

and dismounted. McGivern's gaze moved on, taking in a second, larger ledge somewhat below and well to the left of the first. On the ledge a jumble of monolithic rocks formed a rough circle, as though a giant hand had playfully swiped at the cliff above and hurled down a massive handful to the ledge, afterward carelessly arranging them around a sandy amphitheater. Within this natural cordon was the Apache camp. The pony remuda stood rump to rump along a picket rope strung between two boulders. Supper fires burned by a few brush wickiups, and dusky forms were moving from the camp. This wasn't the main band, that was certain; he counted only a dozen braves.

And no guard on the ridge above. Damn fool young bucks had carelessly deserted their posts to see the wagon, and no doubt would get a fierce castigation from the leader for it. Just now the whole camp was converging on the higher ledge where the wagon had stopped. The white guards were fingering their rifles nervously.

Suddenly one buck wheeled in his tracks, bawled an order. The others halted and straggled sullenly back to camp. The buck who'd given the order went on alone toward the whites. That would be the war chief. McGivern lifted the binoculars and steadied blurrily on the climbing man. He swore softly and fined down the adjustment. The flat cruel features of the Apache swam into focus.

Maco.

Recognition of his old enemy sent a still, quiet hate crawling along McGivern's spine, but his hand held steady, following the war chief's ascent to the ledge. The tall figure of Harlan moved off from the others, and he and Maco met at the juncture of ledge and slope. Words passed. Heated words, for Maco made an angry, slicing gesture with his hand. There was no love lost between these white and Indian renegades; only their dual purpose preserved a thin harmony. Maco had been careful not to let his warriors get near the whites. McGivern thought fleetingly of the Indian youth Gian-nah-tah whose life he had spared, wondered if he was down there in the Apache camp.

Maco ended the caucus by pivoting on his heel and stalking back to his camp. Reggie hesitated a moment, then swung back to his men and barked orders. The crew off-saddled, threw down blanket rolls and gear. Two men unhitched the team, another threw back the tarp on the wagon and lifted out a peeled log roughly the thickness of a corral pole. This he thrust between the spokes of the back wheels, then lashed it securely to the wagon frame. A rough lock, to brake the wagon solidly on the precarious ledge.

McGivern watched them set up camp. Whatever had passed between Harlan and Maco, it was evident that the rifles would not be unloaded tonight. That could be a stroke of luck. McGivern moved the binoculars down, studying the jagged face of the escarpment to the churning river below. Yes, there was the way . . . with Hornbeck's help and the aid of darkness.

He inched back a yard on his belly, rose to his feet and dogtrotted back across the saddle to where Hornbeck and Lissa waited. They had driven the horses to the far end of the cranny. Both squatted on their heels within its mouth. They stirred aside to make room as he sank to his haunches facing them.

"Well?" Hornbeck said impatiently.

"The 'Paches are there, an even dozen. Maco's band, all right. I saw him. But not the main bunch."

"What does that mean?"

"One of two things. Maco's broken with Nachito, which I doubt, or Nachito is holding the rest of the band nearby . . . because Harlan refused to bring his half-dozen men near half a hundred wartailing 'Paches — which was good sense." He paused grimly. "Tall odds for us, all the same. Seven whites, twice that many Apaches."

Hornbeck glanced at Melissa, nervously rubbed his hands together. "What do you have in mind?"

McGivern said flatly, "Those guns have to be destroyed. There's only one way. If we're lucky, we'll only have to take on Harlan's bunch, and we can get the drop on them."

Quietly he outlined it for them. Melissa bit

her lips. "It will be risky . . . for you both. There's no other way?"

"No."

"And I just hold the horses ready — and wait?"

"That's it." He drew the derringer Ma Gates had slipped him from his pocket. "If we don't make it . . . ," he hesitated, ". . . you'll need this."

She took it wordlessly. Hornbeck was pale, but he nodded his determination as he gently pressed her hand. They ate and drank a little from the knapsack, crouching in a tight circle to wait for nightfall. They spoke little except to go over the plan. The cramped inactivity, coupled with bleak anticipation, dragged minutes to eternities. Sunset crowned the heights, rosy strata that faded to gray twilight, then darkness. First moonrise shed a silvery complexion across the rocky landscape; it seemed the dead face of another world, making the tense vigil somehow unreal.

It brought McGivern face to face with the grim riddle of the death he might taste soon. He could cope with the knowledge, as he often had. He could only guess at Hornbeck's thoughts. The sheriff was tense-postured, no hint of hysteria about him. He and Melissa sat close, a wordless communion in that closeness that touched the scout with an unsettling sadness. Strangely, it was not a dead girl for whom his memory fumbled, but a living one. A man might love a memory, but he did not think of death when death was so close.

He remembered Julia as she had looked that day when a casual outing had suddenly become more for them both — the sunlight on her bright hair and the flush of sun and wine in her face and the awakening to a sense of life she had never known. He faced his thoughts with a puzzled self-amazement, a fresh excitement. He had not realized how nearly a hurtful memory had scarred over, yet he could not deny it. *If I come out of this,* he thought, *there'll be time, time to know her.* He'd forgotten how life went quickly on in this new, yet ageless, country of unceasing change.

When he judged that both the Apaches and the Chain Anchor crew were turned into their blankets, McGivern rose and touched Hornbeck's arm. With a half sob Melissa reached up and drew Hornbeck's face to hers; then she was on her feet, groping to the rear of the shadow-blackened niche to lead out the horses.

McGivern went ahead of Hornbeck through the deep vale of shadows that pooled in the saddle dip. They reached the vantage point where he had lain earlier. He sank to a crouch, waiting for Hornbeck to move up beside him. Below the blanketed forms of Harlan's men ringed a large fire. A long guard hunkered down against a wagon wheel, a blanket thrown over his shoulders against the high-country chill. Off to the lower right the Apache camp lay in utter darkness, the cookfires extinguished. The

167

Apaches would have a hidden sentry in camp, but the high location of Harlan's camp would cut off his view, luckily.

McGivern pointed to indicate a shallow arroyo which cut wormlike down the rotted talus of the slope, the alluvial fan at its lower end spilling onto the shale ledge of Harlan's bivouac. Hornbeck nodded his understanding. He was close at McGivern's heels as the scout slipped into the arroyo, flattened himself on its sandy bottom, dug in his elbows and inched his body forward in short lurches. *Lucky it's a white camp we're stalking,* he thought wryly, hearing Hornbeck behind him, breathing heavily, his body scraping along as he clumsily followed McGivern's example.

They stopped just beyond the fitful rim of high-tossed firelight. The back of the wagon was a dozen yards distant; to its left the fire blazed, with its circle of sleeping men. The guard was half dozing against the wheel, his head jerking a little in an unconscious effort to hold to wakefulness, his rifle tipped slackly in his hands.

Signaling to Hornbeck not to move, McGivern came to his feet now, sixgun in hand. He skirted the sleeping men like a flitting shadow, and was halfway around the camp before the guard's head snapped erect at some half-sensed movement. McGivern covered him, raising a finger to his lips. Hornbeck rose, stepped up beside the open-mouthed guard and lifted the rifle from his nerveless fingers. A curt whisper from the lawman ordered the guard down on his face. McGivern moved soundlessly among the sleeping men, collecting their rifles and handguns that lay in sight, tossing these to the soft sand away from the fire.

As he stepped across to the last sleeper, this one suddenly threw his blanket aside and came to a sitting position with a gun in his fist. His mouth opened, hauling in breath to release a shout. With a swift merciless violence, McGivern clubbed the man across the jaw with his Colt, laid him out cold. The crack of metal on flesh and bone brought two others erect in their blankets. They stared, blearily taking this in, then slowly lifted their hands. The remaining three, Harlan included, snored on in their blankets. McGivern was relieved; of them all, only Harlan was likely to resist.

With McGivern covering the crew, Hornbeck pulled out his pocket knife and cut the lashings on the wagon's rough lock. Gingerly he dragged out the log from between the spokes and laid it on the ground. Then he put his shoulder to a rear wheel, gripped the spokes, dug in his heels, and shoved. At McGivern's murmured order, the guard and the aroused sleepers moved over to the wagon with a cowed wariness. With a man straining at each wheel, the wagon budged a few inches, rocked, settled.

"Put your backs into it!" Hornbeck hissed with a savage warning that threw a genuine effort into the other three. The wagon began its soundless roll through the soft sand that covered the ledge rock, slowly at first, then with a ponderous gain of momentum. Harlan grunted in his blankets and settled back with a snoring sigh as McGivern watched unblinkingly. The wagon had reached the outer rim of the ledge, where its pitch took an abrupt plunge. As the front wheels touched the incline, the men leaped away. The heavy wagon careened out over the lip-rock, and then nothing in the world could have stopped it.

There was a moment's silence as the wagon vanished into the darkness below, then a slack, jolting roar as it hit the steep shale beneath and rushed on and downward. McGivern and Hornbeck backed swiftly away toward the upper slope as Harlan and the others rolled out of their blankets. The three who'd helped stared stupidly at the threat of leveled guns in the hands of the pair backing away. With a baffled, bull-chested roar, Harlan was clawing out of his blankets, reaching for a gun that wasn't there. Then the thunderous crash of splitting wood resounded from far below as the loaded wagon hit the lower slope and the river, its destruction muffling its own splash. Harlan stood a stunned moment with the firelight playing on his golden curls; then he lunged for one of the rifles on the ground.

McGivern snapped a shot at him and missed, then wheeled and loped up the arroyo, with the lawman scrambling ahead. Now the guns opened up behind, but the crew was still half blinded by firelight after their rude awakening. Bullets sang off rocks with deep angry whines. For a few seconds Hornbeck and McGivern were highlighted by flickering firelight before they were lost in the deeper shadows upslope.

McGivern heard Hornbeck ahead of him, climbing and panting, then a low groan as Hornbeck's leg buckled under him and he fell. McGivern dragged him to his feet.

"Ricochet — got me in the leg," the sheriff gasped. "Go on."

"Give me your gun and *move!* I'll cover you." McGivern turned as he spoke, firing at the man in the lead as the whole gang poured up the arroyo. The man yelled and shrank against a cutbank. McGivern shot again, and the others scattered behind the rocks. "Go on," McGivern yelled savagely as Hornbeck hesitated.

Hornbeck swore at him, thrust his gun at the scout's hand and resumed his stumbling ascent. McGivern crouched, making himself small between the banks. The bulky figure of Harlan plunged up the arroyo, waving his gun, trying to pull his men into a charge. McGivern fired twice, too hastily. Harlan faltered and cursed blisteringly as he fell back to shelter. Now the bedlam in the Apache camp reached McGivern as a flurry of shouts. He guessed the hostiles' first reaction was that they'd been attacked by Harlan's crew.

McGivern emptied his gun at the rocks below,

then palmed up Hornbeck's and fired again. The Chain Anchor men fired wildly at his gun flashes, but McGivern had already moved to a higher position. Now he could make out a few dusky figures bounding up the moonlit slope off to his right, Maco's gutturals raised in harsh command. The crafty war chief had summed up the situation and was rallying his braves to help the *pinda-likoye* with *pesh-e-gar*, the guns. McGivern turned his attention on the lean, elusive shadows of two Apaches who were bounding like mountain goats ahead of their fellows, up toward the rose-fire winks of McGivern's gun. He turned and raced up the gully, knowing he could not pin down the Apaches as he had Harlan's men.

As he achieved the top of the gully, he saw Hornbeck's limping shape just disappearing into the shadow-filled saddle pass. He'd have to stall pursuit till Hornbeck and Melissa could get a start on horseback. He heard Harlan's crew leave cover and pound up the arroyo.

McGivern pivoted to face the fast-coming Apaches, laying his pistol across his forearm, braced against the uncertain light and a moving target, and steadied down. The .45 bucked against his palm, and the first Apache doubled in midstride and went down.

The second foeman hauled up, nocking an arrow to his gut-strung bow and whipping it level. McGivern fired and knew he'd missed as the Apache, untouched, released his shaft.

It made a close and hateful *whir*, struck an outcrop two feet from the scout's head. For a split second McGivern saw that the arrow had been deflected at an angle — before it ripped sidelong through his hair and scalp. The blinding pain staggered him. His moccasined foot slipped on a smooth shale fragment and turned at the ankle. He tried to twist as he fell sideways, tried to throw out his arms to catch his weight. Something smashed him in the face and he hit the ground, rolling on his back. The stars blazed near, pinwheeled whitely in his blurring eyes, and that was all.

15

A larger blaze that glared and throbbed redly behind his eyelids brought him slowly awake. He knew that he was lying on his back on warm sand with hot sunlight on his face. He remembered with a kind of obscure panic that Apaches would cut off a captive's eyelids and stake him out under the sun. He blinked frantically and found his lashes crusted with blood. He strained them open. The sun, midmorning high, washed with a full painful glare against his sight as he raised his head.

He was in the rock-bounded amphitheater of the Apache bivouac, his wrists tied across his belly. Copper-skinned warriors hunkered in the shade of the monolithic rocks, talking or working on their gear. There was a subdued and ominous quiet about their low gutturals. It hung like a poised knife in the sun-drenched air. Of this he was keenly aware. A youth in his teens, squatting nearby with a rifle across his knees, glanced at McGivern and rose to his feet, then looked at a wickiup a few paces away and grunted a single word: "Maco."

The stiffened hide hinged from a crossbeam over the entrance swung outward, pushed by the war chief's great shoulders as he squeezed through. He stood and was motionless, eyeing McGivern with a contained hatred. He glanced at the young buck. "Go to the camp of *pinda-likoye* with *pesh-e-gar*. Bring the big white-eyes with yellow hair." The youth loped obediently from camp, heading for Harlan's bivouac.

"How do you feel, *Nantan* Day-zen?" Maco's tone bore a cold, cynical edge of humor. He was savoring this moment.

"Well, I thank you." McGivern's reply was even, calm, from a throat parched and swollen. He sat up and covered his painful wince stolidly. He inched his body back against the cool shade of a monolith, only now noting that his feet were tied. He set his teeth against the tortured throbbing of his head. "It is a surprise," he said then. "I had thought your braves would be working on me."

"The *nantan* must have the pleasure of knowing it," Maco said. "Since *Chigo-na-ay's* first beams rose from the desert, my braves have searched by the river. The current is too deep and swift. The *pesh-e-gar* are lost to us. For that, Day-zen, you will scream for death through many days and nights."

"But many white-eyes will live. Can you live with that thought, Maco?"

Maco's smile showed stained and broken teeth. "You will help me bear it, Day-zen. It is a time I have long awaited, that I am not quick to end."

A rattle of shale up the slope announced

Harlan's arrival. He trudged across the camp, stopped a few feet away. "You know, sport, this almost makes losing the guns worthwhile."

"Losing the gun-running, too?" McGivern murmured.

Reggie laughed silently. "Why? You're all here." McGivern's back stiffened, his gaze automatically circled the camp. "Hornbeck and the woman are in one of the *jacales*," Reggie said. "It wasn't hard running 'em to ground after Maco's boys took you, McGivern."

"You fool," McGivern grated flatly. "Have you forgotten she's Belden's wife? With anyone but Maco, she'd be made a slave, not harmed. But Maco! And you turned her over to them . . ."

Irritation shaded Harlan's stare. He shifted his feet uncomfortably. "No choice," he growled. "Maco demanded all three of you. He outnumbers me. Any story'll do for Belden. He'll not be caring, her knowing what she does. Belden had a use for her, but this ends it. Same for Paul. It's too damned bad."

"What about you?"

"How's that?"

"A man who'll run guns to hostiles is low enough," McGivern said steadily, "but I didn't stamp you as one who'd throw a white woman to Maco."

Harlan flushed darkly. "God damn you, McGivern . . . there was nothing else I could do!" His momentary twinge of angry conscience vanished. A cold, vicious brutality that almost matched Maco's supplanted his easy blandness. "You bought into this, McGivern . . . kept poking and prying. And Prentiss had to try blackmail. When her and Hornbeck bought in with you, they earned your rations. Now you can all choke."

With a savage movement, he swung to the war chief. "Let's dicker. I want to be moving out." The two of them talked for a half hour, squatting in front of McGivern, contemptuous of his presence. They made furious ultimatums, swore at each other with the heated arrogance of two overbearing personalities who wouldn't give an ell. McGivern gathered that Harlan wanted to barter directly with Nachito, whom he trusted, but the younger chief was holding the rest of the band out of sight. Harlan's quarrel with Maco yesterday had resulted in the failure to unload the guns, and their subsequent loss. The fact of their double defection worsened their tempers.

Yet they arrived at a compromise. Harlan promised another shipment of two hundred rifles, to be delivered in three months, and got Maco to promise cash on delivery this time, but was unable to wheedle the war chief out of even a quarter payment for the guns McGivern had lost them. McGivern listened with a dull detachment, wondering whether men like these would always stand between the two races and the panacea of brotherhood for which he himself had worked . . . hopelessly, it seemed.

When they had ironed out the last detail,

Harlan rose without a handshake, without a parting word, and tramped from the camp. Maco was scowling with the thought of his commitment as he vanished inside his wickiup. McGivern leaned his aching head against the cool rock and closed his eyes, trying to cudgel his dulled brain. This was a vise of circumstance as hopelessly tight as he'd ever known.

He listened to the sounds of horses moving upslope as Harlan's men broke camp and headed back. He set the ringing hoof falls to a mechanical refrain with the sick beat of blood in his temples. Strangely, the dwindling sound seemed to become louder.

He opened his eyes. The warriors jabbered excitedly as they converged on the east end of the camp. McGivern eased to his feet by straightening his legs and sliding his back up the slippery rock face. He saw the cause of the commotion.

Along the eastward-running wall of the gigantic hogback spine was a crude trail formed by a slipped fault in its bedrock. From where the wall curved out of sight, a line of riders slowly wended single file along the narrow trail coming into the camp. Chiricahua braves . . . ten . . . twenty . . . thirty and more, painted and armed for war. The main body of the band, held at a nearby bivouac till Harlan's men were gone. Like those in camp, the newcomers were young men, many not out of their teens. Yet they were seasoned to the warpath. A few favored badly tended wounds. Some carried Army saddle gear, canteens, cartridge pouches and belts, saddlebags. Others wore Army campaign hats and pieces of uniform. A strutting buck in the lead sported a lance-ripped frock coat and an ancient beaver hat. All carried the Winchester '73's.

As they came off the slope into camp, there was an exchange of joshing camaraderie. Near the end of the long file stepped two horses with the twin poles of a travois litter lashed between them. A youthful brave sat the rocking litter, a slow smile breaking his dark face as the braves began jostling around him, all talking and joking at once. McGivern knew a stunned surprise, almost like a padded blow: the Apache on the litter was the boy he'd saved three days ago, who had neatly turned the tables on him to ride off half dead on a drooping pinto.

Two husky warriors caught Gian-nah-tah's arms, swung him to the ground. He grunted and said something that made them laugh. Maco had emerged from his shelter, his black scowl not breaking as he went over to the youth. They spoke briefly, the youth nodding gravely, stoically facing Maco's angry news.

With a sharp word, he chopped Maco off in mid-speech, and only then looked over at McGivern. Motioning the others about their business, Gian-nah-tah trudged over to where the scout leaned. He walked carefully but erect. He looked exactly as he had three days ago, showing little outward effect from his wound. A fresh calico rag was bound over his midriff, where a poultice made a flat bulge.

"This is not a *nak-kai-ye* stand-off, eh, Day-zen?"

"So," McGivern said coldly, "you are Nachito."

"I did not deceive you." The youth was unsmiling, but his eyes glinted his amusement. "I won the name of Gian-nah-tah at ten summers, when I warned my tribe of a nearby patrol of *rurales* before the scouts saw them. I became a warrior at fourteen, a war chief at eighteen, when alone I slew four white-eyes who came to tear up our land for *pesh-litzogue,* the yellow iron. And with Geronimo, I earned the name of Nachito from the Meh-hi-kanos in Sonora. Did I deceive, Day-zen?"

McGivern shook his head. "Had I known you were Nachito, you would not have escaped so easily."

"This I knew." And now Nachito smiled openly; it did not dull the wicked edge to his next words. "Maco says you came last night with a man and a woman to the camp of the *pinda-likoye* with guns, and those guns lie out of our reach in the river below."

"He speaks straight."

Maco, with a few curious braves straggling behind, had come up and now stood impassively with folded arms. His murky eyes boiled with hate. "Does Nachito question this?" he demanded.

Nachito did not even glance at him, but continued to regard McGivern with curious serenity. "It is known everywhere that Day-zen is a just man. Why did you destroy our guns? Do you not think we have the right to defend ourselves?"

McGivern tilted his head wearily back against the rock. No one knew better the endless record of white treachery that had triggered every Apache atrocity. "Of course you have the right. As it is my right to meet you in the war field, a man against a man. But those who brought the guns were men of my race. Would Nachito crush the snake who warms itself in his blankets?"

"It is a good reason. But in the past you have not fought us this way."

"No." McGivern paused, marshaling himself to speak without emotion. "There was a girl in the land of my youth. She came from where the sun rises, to be my woman. A stagecoach was attacked in the great canyon east of Fort Laughlin. The woman was killed by an Apache lance."

"I remember," Nachito said simply. "The lance was mine."

"You —" McGivern lunged away from the rock. His bound legs twisted beneath him and he fell helplessly on his back at Nachito's feet. A buck leaped forward, his lance lowering its keen tip to McGivern's throat.

"As I do not war on women, my heart was sore," Nachito said quietly. "But as you are my enemy, I tell you to hear me, or die."

"Now or later," McGivern panted. "And I gave you your life. . . ."

"You will listen," Nachito said inexorably. "The soldiers and men of the stagecoach fought furiously before we killed them all. We overturned the coach and set fire to it, and only then heard the white woman cry out. We did not see her lying inside. Maco dragged her out and laughed as he put his torch to her hair. Such, for Maco, is but a beginning. Before he could stop me, I ran my lance through her heart. Since that moment, Maco has hated me." He motioned at the buck, and the lance point was withdrawn from McGivern's throat.

McGivern sat up and felt sweat crawl down his face, felt the shaking of his body with released tension, and did not care that the Apaches saw it. Nor did Maco's scarred face make him hide his grimace of satisfaction. "A man who earns the hatred of Maco sleeps lightly," McGivern said huskily; it was his token of thanks to Nachito.

"A war chief of the *Be-don-ko-he* whose heart turns to water at a white-eyed woman's screams, who admits this to a white-eyes," Maco sneered. "Gladly I took the war trail with Nachito — the grandson of Tana, the lieutenant of Geronimo. If they knew this, both would spit on you."

Nachito turned slowly to face the older man, a hand falling to the hilt of his knife. "They knew," Nachito said softly, "and they did not

182

spit. Perhaps Maco would like to spit."

"I do not spit on crippled boys."

"Then keep it in your mouth with your foolish words. You talk like old Naka-do-klunni, the medicine man. Nobody listens to him but the squaws and the children."

The listening braves grinned; one chuckled aloud and was silenced by Maco's cold glare. McGivern guessed that the co-leadership of this band was an unsatisfactory arrangement for both war chiefs. A note of icy casualness to their insults suggested that they'd quarreled before. Nachito had needed Maco's seniority at first, in winning his reputation with these northern Apaches, but McGivern sensed that there had been a slow shift in the balance of leadership.

The young bucks liked Nachito, with his youth, his humor, and his brash courage. Even his non-Apache quirks, his refusal to torture and his amiable discourse with an enemy, were eccentricities which added to the colorful personality of a born leader. It was Nachito who'd taken the initiative in the gun liaison with Belden. And McGivern guessed that to Nachito's mind Maco had become so much dead wood that the junior chief would be glad of an excuse to sweep out. If Maco had a similar notion, he was stymied by Nachito's popularity. *Maybe*, McGivern thought with the glimmer of a hunch, *just maybe, if I scratch Nachito's back, he'll scratch mine.*

Nachito said thoughtfully, "It is spoken by our brothers at San Carlos that you asked questions.

They told you nothing, yet you learned all!"

"I am called Day-zen."

"Well-named. And now you are here." Nachito regarded him with mock perplexity. "What shall I do with you, Day-zen?"

"He is mine," growled Maco, "as are the other white-eyes. . . ."

"That we shall see," Nachito said serenely. "Have the man and woman brought here."

Three braves loped to a wickiup at the north end of camp. Shortly they returned with Melissa Belden and Paul Hornbeck in tow. One buck forced Melissa to her knees in front of Nachito, his fist fastened in the red-gold mass of her hair. Her clothes were torn and her smudged face bore a dazed, uncomprehending look. Hornbeck's mouth was bleeding; a filthy rag was tied around his thick calf. He kicked furiously at the two Apaches who held his arms. One of them clouted him across the head, and he subsided. The buck who held Melissa jerked her head back at a painful angle, drew his knife and passed it suggestively around the bright tangle of her hair. Nachito spoke sharply, and the buck quit clowning.

"What are these to you, Day-zen?" Nachito asked.

"Friends. The man wears the white-eyes' star of law, the woman is Belden's."

"These things I know. Harlan told Maco that Belden is tired of his woman. She has spirit, to go to war with men. *Enju,* I have need of a ser-

184

vant with spirit." The watching braves grinned and nodded at each other.

"Here you step too far," Maco rumbled. "The woman is mine. Day-zen, too, and the *pinda-likoye* with the star."

McGivern came to his feet now, teetering precariously on his heels and catching his balance. He faced Maco squarely. His heart was trip-hammering with the knowledge that he, Hornbeck, and Lissa had one thin chance for life. It depended on how far Maco could be goaded, on how far McGivern could push a tacit alliance with Nachito. As he felt the Apaches' attention focus upon him, he made his words strong and steady.

"Nachito is hurt. He cannot make a contest. I will fight you, Maco, in the Apache fashion."

Surprise flickered in Nachito's eyes; he said nothing, only watched McGivern intently. A murmur ran through the listening braves. Maco spoke, sneering: "For your freedom, white man?"

"For slavery," McGivern said quietly. "Who would not rather be Nachito's slave than Maco's victim? Then —" he lowered his voice, directing its hard challenge at Maco alone — "we have fought often, you and I, but never as a man facing a man."

"A prisoner does not name terms," Maco growled.

"Our quarrel is not as the quarrel between our people. You know this well."

Excited talk broke out. Who did not know of

185

the almost legendary enmity between Maco and the white-eyed scout? It would be a great thing to witness the final reckoning — a thing of which a man could boast to his grandchildren. McGivern covertly studied the two chiefs, seeing the thoughtful calculation behind Nachito's eyes. If they dueled, and Maco were killed, it would rid Nachito of a powerful enemy-in-rank. The youth's half-friendly feeling for McGivern and sense of obligation for McGivern's sparing his life were of lesser consideration, but not to be discounted either. And it was Nachito's sentiment which could sway the opinion of the braves by a single word.

Maco only saw himself being cheated of torture victims, and this seemed a symptom of his waning power. He tried to salvage face with a half-snarled, "Are these the warriors of the *Be-don-ko-he,* to snivel at the torment of enemies? When you return to your lodges, the women will spit on you and turn from your blankets. Women do not bed with women."

The words were ill-chosen. The excited flurry of talk sweeping the braves became tinged with ugly resentment. Nachito squelched it all by raising his hand. "It is done. Maco shall fight Day-zen, or we will strip him of his weapons and drive him afoot from camp."

The crowd had only needed a single firm ultimatum to crystallize their wavering intent. Nachito, canny politician, had voiced it at the psychological moment. They were solidly behind him now, cheering their approval.

Maco proudly folded his arms, his cruel face stoical. He might win the duel, but he had lost more, and the word would spread through Apacheland . . . Maco would slide into oblivion. Seeing him fearlessly, almost contemptuously, accepting this knowledge, McGivern knew a reluctant admiration for his old enemy.

Nachito drew McGivern aside, pulled his knife and severed the scout's bonds. McGivern stood flexing his cramped muscles, rubbing circulation back to his arms and legs. Nachito eyed him quizzically. "Once more you have done me a service," the young chief said in a low voice. "First you spared my life —"

"And maybe just spared my own," McGivern said dryly, grimly. "As your slave. . . ."

"You can watch for a chance to escape, though you will not escape. Still, I thank you, *pinda-nantan.*"

"That you can prove. I would talk with my friends." Nachito's eyes narrowed, and McGivern knew it was his wits against the war chief's now. He shrugged casually. "Maco may kill me. There is a feeling between me and this man and woman. My last words would be a comfort."

"It is so. If Maco wins, he wins them." Nachito hesitated, touched McGivern's shoulder. "A friend is a good thing. I have many followers, few friends. I did not tell my people how I was shot; they would not understand why you did not kill me. You and I know. Go to your friends, Day-zen."

The braves were all talking at once, hashing over the old quarrel between the duelists, and making bets. McGivern moved over to where Hornbeck and Melissa sat in numb misery in the shadow of an isolated monolith. A single guard squatted by with a rifle.

"I don't understand all this," Hornbeck burst out, motioning at the Apaches. "What's going on, McGivern?"

He hunkered down by them. "Our lives are up for stakes," he said quietly. "I'm going to fight Maco. If I win, the three of us become Nachito's property." He didn't add what would happen if he lost. He glanced now at the Apache guard, a boy of fifteen or so, whose soft face had already seasoned to capable manhood. He was gambling that the lad understood little or no English as, rather than lower his voice and rouse suspicion, he spoke to Melissa in a normal tone. "They find the derringer I gave you?"

Her dazed eyes lifted, her forehead puckering mechanically as though fixing on his words was an effort. "I . . . hid it in my boot. They didn't find it."

"When the fight starts, slip it to Paul. They'll all be watching me and Maco."

"What's on your mind, McGivern?" Hornbeck asked, intent now.

"It's our only way out. I'm going to grab Nachito for a hostage."

16

"If I can kill Maco," McGivern said steadily, "if I can bring him down by Nachito, and get my hands on Nachito before they know what's happened . . . we'll have a chance. Not much, I warrant. But we can't wait."

Hornbeck said hesitantly, "Wouldn't it be better to wait — and lull their suspicions?"

"This may be the only time I'll have my hands free and a knife in them. Nachito's still weak from his wound; he won't fight much. He promised us our lives. But he couldn't keep his braves from your throat or mine for more than a day or so. It's their custom to take only women or children captive. A war party won't be saddled with watching grown male prisoners. And the Apaches know me, consider me dangerous."

Hornbeck was silent for a time, and Mc-Givern gave him unspoken tribute for his poise. The man had unshakably found himself. "All right," he said. "What can I do?"

"Lissa'll give you the pocket pistol. When I grab Nachito, you shoot the guard."

"That boy?"

"Then wing him," McGivern said quietly, insistently, "but get his rifle. If I threaten to kill Nachito, the guard can use the same threat on

189

you two — unless you move first."

Hornbeck wet his lips. "Yes. All right. But if Maco kills you —"

"There's two bullets in the derringer."

"I know. A bullet for me, and. . . ." He swallowed. McGivern's hand went out, gripped his shoulder in a quick hard squeeze. The scout rose and walked through the Apaches, who respectfully made way for him. He halted at the edge of the cleared spot.

Maco was waiting. He'd stripped himself to the waist. He was average height for an Apache — a full head shorter than McGivern — but his broad shoulders and chest swelled with ox-like thews. Sheer strength had long given him the prestige that other war chiefs had won by personality, though he matched any in craft, cunning, and fighting prowess. His obsidian eyes lanced hatred at McGivern and he faintly flexed his long arms, rippling the knotted muscles under his copper hide. McGivern knew he'd have to rely on speed and his knife and try not to close with the Apache, thinking coldly now: *he'd break a man in half if he got his hands on him.*

McGivern shrugged out of his shirt and jacket, tossed them aside. The sun beat against his lean back as he moved toward the middle of the cleared area. The Apaches murmured and pointed at the long knife scar seared into his flesh. Nachito walked out, with the tip of his lance drew a circle roughly fifteen feet in diameter. He lifted two knives from his breechclout and murmured some ceremonial words above them, of which McGivern caught only the last five: "That life may ebb cleanly." He stooped painfully and laid the knives in the center of the circle. Then he walked back to where the warriors were ranked in a ragged cordon around the clearing.

Nachito squatted down a little ahead of the others, and McGivern took note of his position. All of an Apache's training was directed toward vigilance to protect him from surprise; the unexpected caught him completely off guard, undone by his own carelessness. McGivern was depending on the laxity of excitement and the unexpectedness of his move to enable him to seize Nachito, hold him helpless before the braves could rally.

Sunlight pooled wickedly along the waiting blades. The adversaries wove warily toward the weapons from opposite sides, an easy grace to the mincing shift of their moccasined feet. McGivern moved first, lunging, stooping and picking up a knife, in the same movement flicking out a foot to kick Maco's knife away. It slid only about a foot. Maco, moving with surprising agility, dipped a long arm and snatched up the knife at the same time leaping aside to escape the vicious orbit of steel swung at his shoulder by McGivern. Pivoting gracefully on a heel, Maco countered with a straight-arm lunge that carried his pointed knife over McGivern's shoulder as the scout ducked. He tried to whip under Maco's guard, to slash at his abdomen, and again Maco leaped back.

Now Maco moved in on him, his knife making wide glittering arcs at the end of his long arm, holding McGivern off and at the same time forcing the scout back step by step to the circle of bystanders. McGivern must either leap aside or meet the attack. With a lightning kick to Maco's thigh, he sent the Indian reeling back a pace and then lunged to meet him. He ducked beneath Maco's full-armed swing, again sought to bring his blade up under Maco's guard.

The Apache's free hand clamped powerfully over McGivern's knife wrist. As Maco's knife swung back, McGivern flung his left arm around the Apache's waist, lifted, threw his hip behind Maco's right buttock, and swung him off his feet. Maco crashed on his back, but still held McGivern's wrist. He fought to pull McGivern on top of him; the scout stiffened his legs, braced wide, and Maco gave up. He swung his knife at McGivern's leg. McGivern jerked the leg away, and it threw him off balance. He kicked blindly at Maco's hand, and the knife flew from it, the point burying itself in the earth eight feet away.

But the maneuver let Maco give a powerful tug on McGivern's wrist that brought the scout down onto him with a grunting impact. Maco's long arms whipped around him like crushing snakes. His left hand still holding McGivern's wrist pulled the scout's own knife against the small of his back, point outward. McGivern was on top, but helpless . . . and now Maco had the hold he had feared. The tremendous power of his arms tightened, straining, until McGivern felt his breath choke in his throat. His ribs constricted against his lungs; bright lights exploded in his eyes.

Savagely he bent his head, fastened his teeth in Maco's shoulder, bit through the flesh and hung on. The war chief squirmed, making no sound, but McGivern felt the pain loosen Maco's arm grips. Throwing all his strength into the effort, McGivern pulled his knife hand free, whipped it beneath Maco's body. The Apache grabbed at the wrist again, awkwardly, but now the knife was at *his* back, flattened against the flesh. He tried to tug it away; McGivern hung on. He could have turned the blade into Maco's back, but an icy warning beat through his red fury: *get him by Nachito first.*

He heaved sideways and they rolled, Maco on top for an instant, but McGivern throwing his weight up and rolling again, using the impetus to roll them both over a third time, locked together, till they lay on their sides not two feet from where Nachito squatted.

For a moment it was almost as though they were resting, gathering strength, strained chest to chest. Not once had McGivern relaxed his jaws on Maco's shoulder. Now McGivern relentlessly turned the knife, the razored steel breaking flesh. McGivern's biting hold practically immobilized Maco's upper body, yet he strained awkwardly to tug McGivern's hand from his back, his own right arm keeping its crushing hug on the scout's body. McGivern now thrust with all his power, felt steel grate against a rib and slip past, and then the blade sank to the hilt. Blood gushed warmly over his hand.

Maco's bull-like frame stiffened, heaved with a mighty spasm that jolted loose McGivern's hold and flung him on his back by Nachito's knees. He still held to the knife, and he pulled savagely, and it stuck. He wrenched and twisted, Maco's body turning with the pull, and the blade slipped free. The war chief's legs twitched once; then his great carcass was motionless.

Sucking in a deep breath, McGivern sat up slowly, as though fully spent with the effort. Then, before the awed braves could even begin to react from the tensely stiff spell that bound them, his hand shot out, closed on Nachito's throat, and yanked powerfully. McGivern's legs thrust up, bringing him to his feet and dragging Nachito up with him. He swung the young war chief around, back to him, wrapped his left arm around Nachito's neck and locked him helplessly. His right hand held the point of his wet knife against Nachito's throat just under the ear.

The braves were utterly stunned, paralyzed for the moment, as McGivern had known they would be. He had to move only a few steps to put his back against a towering rock slab at one side of the circle. As he swung his back against it, he rapped into the silence: "A move — the smallest move — and he dies."

Then the cracking bark of the derringer. Hornbeck had waited almost too long.

The shot brought the Apaches to their senses; Nachito was the first to recover. He strained his body away from McGivern's, his hand tugging at McGivern's deathlike grip. The scout ground his elbow cruelly into the youth's wound, and Nachito, too weak to resist, relaxed shudderingly.

A wicked murmur of sound, like a rising storm, swept through the warriors; through the stir of dusky bodies, McGivern saw the boy guard on the ground, clutching a bloody shoulder. Hornbeck had already snatched up the rifle and leaped in front of Melissa.

McGivern sent his words flat and cold across the rising voices: "A move, I said, and Nachito dies. Hear me, men of the *Be-don-ko-he*. One of you will get our horses . . . the rest stand as you are. We will ride from here, taking Nachito with us. When we reach the white man's town, Nachito will be freed."

A wrenched laugh gurgled from Nachito's throat. "Day-zen is a fox, but the *Be-don-ko-he* are not rabbits to leap to his bidding. Brothers, you have guns. Shoot him through my body."

"Maco is dead," McGivern cried out challengingly. "If Nachito dies, who will lead you?"

"*Tah-zay*," Nachito gasped. A lanky warrior who towered inches above his fellows took a hesitant step forward. "Careful," McGivern murmured.

"Tah-zay," Nachito said. "To you — my friend — I have told my plans and hopes for the people. Kill Day-zen and lead the way."

Tah-zay's wiry arm moved in protest. "The plans were yours, *sheekasay*. I cannot lead. The feeling of the men is for you." The braves murmured their agreement.

Nachito gave a strangled cry, and McGivern felt the keen disgrace of this tremor through the war chief's body. "Nachito has been tricked like a child that rides the *tsoch* on its mother's back. I am not fit. *Shoot!*"

"Hornbeck." McGivern raised his voice. "The tall Indian. Put your gun on him." The lawman butted the rifle to his shoulder and sighted along Tah-zay's back. "Yes, shoot," McGivern gibed. "We will die, so will Nachito; and his plans will die with Tah-zay. Is there another among you who can lead as Nachito hopes?"

A warrior at the edge of the throng suddenly moved, shadow-silent, slipping behind a near rock. "Stop that man," McGivern said sharply, knowing the Apache meant to get above him.

"Pi-on-sen-ay," Tah-zay shouted. "Come back! The craft of Day-zen is as ours." The warrior must have hesitated, for Tah-zay cursed him. "Spawn of a coyote, I do not fear to die — *but Nachito must live.*"

Pi-on-sen-ay came into sight off a rock, dropping like a cat back to the ledge. He said sullenly, "You take the word of a white-eyes?"

"Of this white-eyes alone. Is there an Apache

who does not know the heart of Day-zen? Once at San Carlos, my mother, Tes-al-bes-tin-ay, was near to death; it was Day-zen who brought the white-eyed medicine man who cured her." His gaze leveled on McGivern. "You will let Nachito go?"

"I gave the promise. Are Tah-zay's ears bad?"

"Pi-on-sen-ay, bring three horses." At Tah-zay's quiet command, a groan rose deep from Nachito's chest. "Be still," McGivern whispered. "You will be a child in truth if you cannot take defeat like a man."

Pi-on-sen-ay went to the picket line and led back the horses. He left them between Mc-Givern and the crowd, reins trailing. McGivern called to Hornbeck to bring Melissa and circle widely around the Apaches, keeping his rifle ready, and mount up, after catching up the reins of McGivern's horse.

Only when this was done did McGivern push away from the rock. His knife did not leave Nachito's throat. He moved to his own rangy sorrel. As he quickly brought his knife hand down to lift Nachito's foot to stirrup, the war chief tried feebly to wrench away. In a flash, with Nachito stirruped, McGivern lifted him bodily into the saddle, at the same time swinging up behind, his knife at Nachito's ear again. It was accomplished smoothly in the space of a few seconds, before anyone knew what was happening.

He kneed the sorrel lightly. It followed Hornbeck's mount, the sheriff guiding both horses.

All the way for the length of the slope above the camp, McGivern's back crawled, expecting any moment the smash of an arrow or a bullet as some impulsive brave broke. But only Maco could have rallied them to sacrifice Nachito, and Maco was dead. The camp lay silent and unmoving behind. . . .

McGivern realized how deep-seated was the voluntary loyalty of these braves toward their leader. Only a dozen years ago, Nachito would have been another Mangus Colorado or rankling, such a one as this could be the rallying point for Victorio or Cochise — a personality like a living flame, which could draw followers from beyond his own tribe. Even now, with old hatreds still rankling, such a one as this could be the rallying point for hundreds of young Apaches . . . and another interlude of bloody and hopeless warfare.

It cannot, it must not happen, McGivern thought, and the thought stayed with him. He knew what he would have to do, soon, after Nachito was released.

Once they had reached the upper ridge with its saddle framed pass, McGivern quickened pace. He knew that the Apaches would follow, that they would have an unseen escort for many hot, dry miles. He only hoped they could reach Saguaro before nightfall.

"You had better be sure, very sure," Belden said softly.

"Hell," Harlan answered irritably, "I left all three in Maco's hands. Man, he's an Apache."

"So is McGivern, very nearly."

Reggie grunted, slacked back in his chair with his legs crossed, thumbs hooked in his belt. It had been the work of fifteen minutes for Hosmer, the ranch blacksmith, to liberate Belden when Harlan and the crew had returned to find him handcuffed to his bed. Afterward the crew threw a drunken spree, Harlan warning them to confine it to the ranch. He and Belden had ridden to town and the seclusion of Belden's freight office to discuss what had happened and weigh their future moves.

"At least," Belden had told him, "you were wise to turn Paul and Lissa over to Maco. It saves us a nasty job. With what they know, neither would be useful now; on the contrary, they're dangerous."

Looking at the fat man now, sprawled like an immobile toad in his chair, the lamp on the desk between them throwing Belden's features into weird relief, making them agelessly craggy and evil, Harlan knew a full resurgence of his hatred. He couldn't deny that he himself had taken the easy way of handing the sheriff and Melissa to the Apaches, but McGivern's condemnation had stung. Belden hadn't even a twinge of regret. He hated the fat man the more for being able to escape living with his acts.

"So nothing's changed?" Reggie asked softly.

"Nothing. Learn to accept what happens, my

boy. The loss of Paul and Melissa is merely an irritant which can be hurdled. Meanwhile, you did well, bluffing Maco into promising cash on delivery. A letter to my brother in New Orleans will resume the gun traffic."

Reggie hesitated. "Maybe we'd better soft-pedal it awhile. If McGivern sent what he learned on to the Army. . . ."

"It will prove nothing, in itself. One man's words — discredited by the fact that he is a murderer who broke jail and forced the sheriff to leave with him. Neither are heard of again. What does that prove? Nothing. McGivern's friends will need more than that to launch a Federal inquiry. Now kindly get out of here. I have work to do."

He bent his head over some papers; it was as though Reggie had ceased to exist. Harlan rose, opened the door, and carefully slammed it behind him as he went out. He grinned with a truant boy's satisfaction as he groped his way through the darkened outer office. Outside, he went to his horse, mounted, and swung toward the archway.

Abruptly he pulled the reins and brought the animal to a halt. He pulled back into the shadows of the high fence, his heart pounding with a scared savagery that left him faint. The archway was wide, allowing anyone just inside to gain a full view of the street for a block in either direction. A first fleeting glimpse of the south end had shown him three riders coming in. An orange outwash of light from a store window had picked out the three plainly.

McGivern. Hornbeck. Melissa. Hanging with weariness across their drooping horses . . . *but alive and well.* All of them.

After the initial presence of mind that led his retreat to shadows, Reggie's brain drew a numbed blank. Then it functioned chaotically, first with the impulse to shoot McGivern and the sheriff as they drew abreast of the archway. He saw the madness of that notion as it occurred.

What to do; stay and bluff it out? He rejected that at once; he'd never feared any man, but he suddenly feared McGivern with a clammy and paralyzing fear. There was something unresistible about a man who could free himself and two others from a camp of armed Apaches. What had gone wrong, he did not know. He did know with an iron certainty that McGivern had effected it.

He let out a long, sighing breath of relief as McGivern and Hornbeck did not turn in at the archway, but continued downstreet. *But they've seen the light in the Old Man's window, sure as hell. They'll come here for George. All he can tell them is you left a while ago. If they look for you, it'll be at the ranch.*

The thought steadied him. George was through, with three witnesses to the illicit gun traffic. But he, Reggie Harlan, could get out of this with a sizable stake if he played his hand cooly. . . . There was at least ten thousand dollars in Belden's office safe, and it was a week's

201

ride to the Mexican border. Plenty of country for a man to lose himself in.

He cursed softly, then, remembering that he didn't know the combination of the safe. He could go in and put a gun on George and force him to open it, but McGivern and the sheriff might come in at any moment. He would wait until they had taken Belden and left . . . then open the safe. How?

Black powder. There were three kegs in one of the yard sheds, and he'd seen safes blown open by experts in his younger, wilder days. He'd tether his horse at the rear of the yard where there was a gate in the back fence. Crack the safe . . . dump the paper money in a sack . . . get out through the rear office window . . . circle the sheds and reach his horse by the time the first spectators were drawn by the explosion.

He put his horse across the yard toward the isolated shed where explosives were kept. From its door he could see by the street lights anyone who came or left through the front archway.

Once in the shed, he lighted a lantern, closed the door, and kept his eye close to a knothole facing the yard as he set about opening a powder keg with a crowbar. He smiled thinly, thinking of the family fortune he'd rejected years ago. Really, it was the tag of pompous responsibility he'd have had to assume with it that he'd rejected . . . Ten thousand to spend as he pleased in the land of *mañana* was better than a million in a social straightjacket.

17

All three of them had breathed easier when the lights of Saguaro grew into view across the flats. It was late darkness, long after twilight. Hornbeck and Melissa were swinging numbly, half dead with exhaustion, to their horses' mechanical gait. McGivern could feel his own trained vitality sapped to its limit by the ordeal of the past two days.

The closeness of town summoned a spark of outrage to Hornbeck's words as he returned to the bitter controversy that had divided them an hour ago. McGivern had set Nachito afoot and the young chief had headed back north across the tawny flats to meet his warriors, invisible on the backtrail.

"I'll give it to you once more," McGivern said wearily. "I had to keep my promise to free Nachito. There was something bigger at stake than my word of honor. . . ."

"A thin argument — that he'd be martyred in a white man's jail," Hornbeck flared back.

"He would, though. . . . Years ago, Mangus Colorado, big chief of the Mimbrenos, went alone to the diggings of some white prospectors and told them in a nice way to move on, out of Apache country. They tied him up and whipped him almost to death. He lived to start the first of the Apache wars, and men from every Apache tribe followed him. Later, when Mangus Colorado surrendered to white soldiers, they shot him down in cold blood. And that set off the worst uprisings of all . . . took twenty years to put down. To a broncho Apache, jail is as disgraceful as a whipping, worse than death." McGivern paused pointedly. "If you didn't see — back there — that Nachito is the same kind of leader, you're blind."

"But this is 1881. The Apaches are on reservation, except for a few renegade bands like Geronimo's."

"And Nachito's. And the hundreds of young men who'd break away to follow him. Why trade for that many rifles unless he had more braves lined up . . . reservation bucks ready to break at a word from him? Jailing him would have the same effect as jailing Mangus Colorado, just possibly worse. There's something else, too. Day-zen — me — is one of the few whites who's always treated honestly with the Apaches. If I'd failed to release him, it would have been a master stroke of betrayal by the white-eyes. In some ways they're like children . . . if complete confidence in a man's honor is childlike. They depended on me to keep my word — or else none of us would be alive."

"But Nachito will go on," Hornbeck said doggedly, "to raid and kill again. Good God, McGivern, after what you told me about your fiancee, how can you give those devils an inch of advantage? Even granted what you said, that Nachito is the man to draw hundreds behind him?"

"That'll take time," McGivern said grimly. "He'll lose face for a while, when it gets around how I tricked him and took him as a live hostage from forty of his fighting men. Not for long, but long enough for me to get information to Colonel Cahill that will stir the top brass to sending hundreds of troops into the field to round up the renegades. I'll offer my services as scout free. I know some now about how Nachito's mind works . . . and that's half the battle won. I'll chase him and harry him, give him time to do nothing but run till he's cornered. It'll be a lesson no Apache will forget."

Hornbeck lapsed into gloomy silence, and there was only the thin *clop* of horses' hoof falls through the darkness, nearing town. McGivern thought back with a sad dispirit to Nachito's last words before they'd parted: "You were right to call me *ish-kay-nay*, a boy, when first we met, Day-zen. See how you have foxed the boy."

"Then now I call you man," McGivern had replied gruffly. "You had not tasted defeat, and it made you careless. A man gains by every mistake. Soon you will see the greater mistake of your father, and his, in fighting the *pinda-likoye*. When the Apaches were many and the white-eyes few, your greatest chiefs could not drive them out. Now the white-eyes are many, and

205

Nachito is playing a fool's game. When he knows this, he will go to the reservation and lead his people in the ways of peace and change."

"The ways of our fathers were good," Nachito had said angrily. "What right have the *pinda-likoye* to force their ways on us?"

"The right of might," McGivern had replied wearily, "and of broken treaties and crooked agency men and other treachery. These things will pass with time. You cannot change them by more killing."

"Then I can die fighting their wrongness," Nachito had said bitterly. "It is too bad, Day-zen. It was near my heart that we were almost *nejeunee,* friends."

"Yes." These were their last words, and Nachito was gone, back to his brave and hopeless fight against history.

Now as they rode through the first rectangles of light thrown from windows onto the soft dust of the street, Melissa released an audible sigh. Even McGivern felt a faint sense of home-coming.

Yet he pushed the thought of Julia Lanphere back in his mind. Belden had to be taken. Automatically he glanced across the board fence that skirted the freight yard, seeing the light in the high front window of the office.

Hornbeck followed his glance and said, "Not without me you don't. I'm taking Melissa to the hotel first. Belden is my job."

Mine, McGivern corrected grimly, but not aloud. They rode on to the livery stable and left their horses, evading the startled hostler's questions. By now the whole town knew that the sheriff had ridden away early yesterday with a shackled prisoner in tow. A small crowd gathered behind the three of them as they crossed to the hotel. Hornbeck, limping a little, was supporting Melissa with an arm around her waist as they went inside. McGivern halted in the doorway, turning to face the townsmen. "Go on about your business, you people."

They took in his gaunt height and trail-stained clothes, the harried warning in his face. They slowly dispersed, muttering sullenly. He waited on the porch till Hornbeck came back, and without a word the two men went to the sheriff's office. Hornbeck buckled on a spare shell belt and gun, and found an extra .45 which he loaded and handed to McGivern, who shoved it in his belt. Then they angled downstreet toward the freight office, McGivern slowing his pace to accommodate Hornbeck's limp. "Better see a doc."

"Afterward," was Hornbeck's stubborn reply.

They went through the archway, crossed the yard, and went up the steps. "I know the office," Hornbeck murmured, stepping ahead of McGivern. He softly opened the door and eased into the outer office, guiding McGivern with a hand on his wrist. They moved across the murky dimness till McGivern heard the lawman grip a doorknob and turn it. The door opened into a short corridor; at its end, a crack of light showed beneath a door. Hornbeck's gun whispered from leather, and McGivern palmed his own and moved after him.

Hornbeck opened the door suddenly and kicked it wide; it crashed with a pistol-shot impact against the wall. Belden sat behind his desk. His face was like a grotesque totem carving, showing nothing at all. The flame of the desk lamp guttered faintly in the draft, exaggerating the shadows to weird, wavering patterns. The air of this musty little cubbyhole was stifling and motionless; it was like a den where some malign being conjured dark spells against mankind.

They stepped into the room and moved tacitly apart. Hornbeck rapped crisply, "On your feet, George. I'm holding you for the United States Marshal."

"Why, that fool. That blundering, swaggering fool," Belden said almost pleasantly, and McGivern knew he meant Harlan.

A desk drawer was open at the fat man's elbow. With incredible swiftness his small hand blurred down and dipped a small-caliber gun from the drawer, fired. The hasty shot whipped between the standing men. McGivern's hand lashed out and batted Hornbeck's gun down as the sheriff fired, the roar of his gun merging with McGivern's own.

Belden plunged backward like a dying buffalo, his swivel chair skidding away from its occupant's tilting weight. The room trembled with the impact of his fall. McGivern skirted the desk, looked, and rammed the gun back in his belt. Hornbeck came around beside him, finally dragged his hot-eyed glance to meet McGivern's.

"Why did you knock my gun down?"

"I thought you might have forgot he was Melissa's husband."

Hornbeck slowly holstered his gun, staring bitterly down at the bloated hulk whose gaudy waistcoat clashed with a deep ugly stain, whose bulbous eyes were frozen in the iced-dead stare they had worn in life. "No," he said hollowly. "No, I didn't forget."

"Better see the doc now," McGivern suggested. He turned quietly and left the office. It was Hornbeck's job now, his to finish. His somehow to whip the long-compromised townsmen into a posse and clean up the leaderless riff-raff at Chain Anchor. McGivern's job was done, and the single-minded intensity that had burned in him these many months drained away. About Belden he felt no regret. He had warred on and killed Apaches who deserved better. . . .

He stood a full minute on the porch, breathing a hot wind off the desert, with its myriad of clean smells. Then he turned out of the yard and headed for the hotel. He was aware of the rancid sweat and filth that caked his body. The aftertaste of grime that summed up this whole job was strong in his mind, and maybe cleansing his body would help. Yet he came abreast of the Belle Fourche, and a sudden impatience to see Julia, hear her voice, turned him through the swing doors.

He heard her before he saw her — sitting on the bar with a hand on her hip and teamsters and cowhands ringing her with rapt attention as she sang. He went to the bar, leaned against a deserted end and watched her till her head turned toward him. Her face went white; her eyes widened, dark with the residue of some unguessable strain. Her voice broke in mid-note. He smiled, and nodded assurance. She picked up the thread of her song again. When it was ended, the men overrode her protests, demanded more. She shrugged a little, smiled her resignation at McGivern, and began singing again.

He listened, toying with a drink he didn't want, thinking sleepily of what he wanted to say to her and wondering how to begin. His head began to tilt unconsciously.

The roar of a muffled explosion shuddered across Julia's voice, and she broke off. The whole building trembled. A babble of talk started as men broke for the door. McGivern was first through the batwings, veering in his run to meet Hornbeck limping from the doctor's office by the hotel.

"What is it?"

"Don't know," Hornbeck grunted over his shoulder. "Sounded like it was from the freight yard . . . but I just left there, and nobody. . . ."

His voice trailed off as McGivern raced ahead in long, loping strides. Smoke was pouring from a broken window of the freight office building. *From Belden's room,* McGivern thought, and was lunging for the porch when he braced swiftly to a stop. A man, something bulky dangling from his hand, was dashing across moonlit patch of ground at the rear of the building, to vanish in a shadowy tangle of sheds.

McGivern ran after him, tugging the gun from his belt. He saw the running man dart between two sheds and break for an open space beyond, clearly highlighted by moonglow. A horse stood tethered against the back fence that hedged the yard, and the man headed for it. McGivern pounded after him and the man heard him and wheeled around so quickly he stumbled. He caught his balance and McGivern saw the light strike off his gun as he swung it up. His hat rolled off with his sharp turn and the moonlight silvered his golden hair.

McGivern stopped. A dozen yards separated them. He called: "Harlan!"

The man's great shoulders hunched high and stiff with surprise; he cursed in recognition. An orange tongue of flame spewed hip-high to his big body. McGivern felt the bullet furrow hotly along his lifting forearm. But his arm continued to lift, holding steady till Harlan's hulking upper body blacked the sights of his sixgun. He squeezed the trigger as Harlan's gun bellowed again.

Harlan was jolted back two steps and then he braced his legs apart, still clutching the sack in his left hand as his right arm chopped up and down, firing again and again as though he were throwing each shot in his fury. McGivern felt a numbing blow in his shoulder, but he kept his feet and aimed again carefully and shot. Harlan's whole body shuddered with the hit. His gun fell to his side. He took a single long, almost careful-seeming, step forward and then his footing skidded away and he plunged face first in the dust. It moiled up around him in a silvery haze and settled thinly.

McGivern walked to him, reached out with a toe and stirred the sack away from Harlan's out-flung hand. It fell open and spilled out packages of greenbacks. He knelt and picked one up, hefting it gently in his palm before he dropped it by the dead man. He said aloud, yet softly, "You bought it all, you and Belden. Every damned cent's worth."

"I'm glad you told me about Clyde," Julia Lanphere said quietly.

He looked at her across the table. He had been thinking that the dark dress she wore was like a mourning gown, and her words startled him. "Glad?"

"Perhaps that was a poor thing to say . . . but I've felt so guilty, terribly guilty . . . that I sent

212

him to his death when I asked his help. I thought he'd been caught in an attempt to gather evidence for us. When you told me what Harlan said about his attempt to blackmail the gunrunners — no doubt using that same evidence — well, it was a relief."

McGivern lightly, restlessly rubbed his bandaged shoulder where Harlan's bullet had made a trifling flesh wound. "I thought maybe you and Prentiss. . . ."

She looked at him quickly. "No." A sadness shaped her mouth. "I am sorry for Clyde, truly sorry. Perhaps he took too much for too long off bigger men, until it warped his better feelings. Or . . . he wanted to marry me. Perhaps he thought the blackmail money would persuade me. But even if I hadn't known, I would have told him no."

They were sitting in the deserted Belle Fourche. It was still early in the morning, but McGivern had already said his farewells to Paul Hornbeck and Melissa Belden. Hornbeck meant to finish out his term of office here, he had said — do his best to clean up the corruption that Belden had sowed. Meanwhile he'd personally clarify the testimony at the inquest for Clyde Prentiss, and McGivern was free to go.

"You'll get small thanks from the town," McGivern had advised him. "They've lived on their knees to Belden too long."

"So did I," Hornbeck had said quietly. "I

213

won't do it for thanks; it just has to be done. After that, we'll go to Georgia and see about some land holdings Lissa's family owned. It may be a start. We're going to try."

And Melissa's face had been drawn and worn, yet with a composed happiness overlaying it. "We're not deceived that it will be easy, Tom. But we can do it." She'd added, almost defiantly, "Do you think we have that right?"

"You have every right," McGivern had said.

Afterward he had gone to the Belle Fourche, where Ma Gates had said a warm good-bye, then discreetly left McGivern and Julia alone.

Out of the deep reserve of his lifetime, McGivern had to struggle for words. No matter how he framed what he wanted to say, he thought that it would sound too bald for the occasion. So much had happened. There was Clyde Prentiss, among other things. Without knowing whether he was acting wisely, he'd told her about Clyde. And felt a strong relief at her reaction. Yet he had no certainty of her real feelings, and he told himself heavily, *maybe you're just a damned fool. You still need more time.*

He pushed his chair back and stood, saying, "I've got to be going. It's a long way to the fort."

Julia rose too and followed him out to the tie rail. The sorrel, inexhaustibly rugged and rested now, pricked up its ears eagerly. McGivern stepped up into the saddle and looked down at Julia. She reached out and laid a hand on the sorrel's shaggy mane. "How long will you be gone?"

She expects me to come back. He felt a little foolish, and suddenly good. "We may be in the field a long time, rounding up Nachito. Weeks, months maybe."

She said gently: "We're not just two lonely people grabbing at straws, Tom. I know that — and so do you. When you come back it will be easier. We'll have the time then, and the words." She paused, her eyes bright again, and proud. "Go along, Tom, and God bless you."

The sorrel sensed its rider's mood and pranced foolishly the whole length of the street. McGivern's shoulder caught an aching twinge with each strike of the hoofs, but he gave the animal its head.